Spring-Heeled Jack: Man or Fiend

By Charlton Lea

Penny Dreadful Press Vol. 2

Compiled by Joseph A. Lovece

IMPORTANT.

Every Reader should procure at once the

FOUR NEW NUMBERS

OF THE

DETECTIVE TALES

Dealing with the adventures and hair-breadth escapes of some of the World-famous Sleuth-Hounds.

THE NEW NUMBERS ARE ENTITLED

325. A FIGHT FOR A MILLION
326. A ROGUE'S DISCOMFITURE
327. THE GREAT TRUNK MYSTERY
328. SILVER-TONGUED SID

Each Volume is Complete in itself and contains 80 Pages.

NOW READY.   **PRICE TWOPENCE.**

"ALL BRITISH" PICTURE . . POST CARDS .

Six Cards in each Set.

Ask your Newsagent to show them to you.

Are the Latest and Most Artistic Series of Picture Post Cards.

QUEENS OF HEARTS.   MOTOR SERIES.   SING-SONG SERIES.
QUEENS OF SPORT.   RIGHT-ON COMICS, No. 1.
FOOTBALL SERIES.   DOGS AND THEIR OWNERS.
RIGHT-ON COMICS, No. 2.   RIGHT-ON COMICS, No. 3.

Six Cards for Sixpence.

If you cannot procure these splendid Cards in your district, send Twelve Halfpenny Stamps and the Set you choose will be forwarded, post free, from the Aldine Publishing Co., Ltd., 1, 2, & 3, Crown Court, Chancery Lane, London, W.C.

MAN OR FIEND

OR, THE FIRST APPEARANCE OF SPRING-HEELED JACK.

By CHARLTON LEA,

Author of "The Dick Turpin Tales," "The Claude Duval Library," "The Mysteries of Newgate," etc., etc., etc.

CHAPTER I.

Accused, Disgraced, Dishonoured, and Condemned to Death.—The Escape.

"So you are back again from gay France?"

"Gay! A nation cannot be called gay when every mouth speaks of war; when every man shrugs his shoulders and points to these cliffs. Hubert, all France is dazzled with Bonaparte's victory. Austria is at his feet. 'Conquete de la Haute Egypte' is graven on his sword, and ere long his studied insults will provoke England to arms again."

The two men, young Lieutenant Bertram Wraydon, and his half-brother, Hubert Sedgefield, sat at the window of an hotel.

Wraydon had gone to Paris to enjoy himself and look about him generally, but his time of leave had expired, and his regiment of Hussars, lying at Colchester, claimed his services.

"A gloomy outlook," Sedgefield remarked, pushing back his dark, flat hair. "Well, Wraydon, you chose the army for the purpose of getting shot or sabred, I suppose. Pshaw! seeking bubble reputation at the cannon's mouth is but a poor game, after all. I," with an uplifting of his heavy eyebrows and a pull at his sharp, protruding chin, "am glad that I looked no further than my law-books. You have heard that I got through my examinations and am in practice now?"

"Yes. Let me congratulate you."

"Rather let me congratulate a young man who finds himself with ten thousand a year and a snug estate," Sedgefield returned.

A smile lit up Bertram Wraydon's face.

"If I get shot or sabred, all will be yours," he said.

"So!" Hubert Sedgefield drew his finger and thumb down his sallow cheeks. "Yes, so it is willed; but, to tell you the truth, I have no ambition to be a rich man. Were I so, I should grow lazy, useless, and a curse to myself. Well, Bertram, where have you bestowed your baggage?"

"Marcus Tench, Colonel Manfred's body-servant, is looking after it for me."

"Ah! I had forgotten you met Colonel Manfred in Paris," Sedgefield remarked, holding his wine-glass up to the light.

"Yes. He took great pains to make my visit a pleasant one, and showed me many places of interest," Bertram Wraydon replied. "Indeed, it seemed as if he had sought me out, instead of meeting me by accident."

"Colonel Manfred is a noble-hearted man," Sedgefield said, bringing the glass to the level of his lips. "He was my father's best friend, and the adviser of my boyhood's days. But," leaning out of the window, "what is this? Here come the colonel and his servant, with some of the Prevention men with him."*

"They seem to be quarrelling about something," Wraydon remarked, turning his eyes in the same direction.

They came up, striding into the hotel, up the stairs, and presently into the room where Wraydon and Sedgefield were sitting at their wine.

Colonel Manfred, a tall, grizzled man, was pale and sternly sad. Tench, his servant, a man with sunken eyes, high cheek-bones, and a long upper lip, stood at attention, and the Prevention men, in their queerly-shaped glazed hats, short jackets, knee-breeches, and buckle-shoes, gazed solemnly first at Bertram Wraydon and then at Hubert Sedgefield.

"It was no fault of mine, sir," Tench said, turning to Lieutenant Wraydon. "They insisted on opening your despatch-box."

"Well, I suppose it is not smuggling for a man to carry his private letters about with him," Bertram said, laughing.

"Lieutenant Wraydon," Colonel Manfred said, "this is a very serious business. The Prevention men found documents of a very incriminating character in your despatch-box.

---

* A body of men whose duty it was to hunt down smugglers; afterwards called coastguards.—ED.

Heaven help me! what persuaded you to take a bribe from the French?"

"A bribe?" exclaimed Wraydon, starting up.

"Ay, sir," said the leader of the Prevention men. "Here are your instructions," holding up a closely-folded paper. "From what I can make out, you have agreed to supply a plan of the fortifications of Dover."

"Are you mad? I know nothing of this!"

"Mad or not," said the Prevention man, "I shall take you into custody, and charge you with being a spy."

Stricken dumb at the accusation, Bertram Wraydon felt the room going round with him. His chest rose and fell, and his breath came and went with a sobbing sound.

"A spy!" he gasped out at length—"a spy!"

"Lieutenant Wraydon," said Colonel Manfred, his voice hoarse with emotion, "in one of these documents Silas Plyers, the outlaw and renegade, is mentioned. It would appear that you have been acting in concert with him."

"A lie! A base conspiracy! These documents are forgeries!" Wraydon cried, wildly.

"That remains to be seen," Colonel Manfred said. "There is such a thing as King's Evidence, and Plyers may be persuaded to come over. The officers must do their duty. Wraydon, this is too terrible to contemplate. Heaven send that you may be able to explain it away!"

* * * * * *

The court-martial found him guilty, and he was a doomed man. It seemed too horrible to be true. Was there no such thing as justice in heaven or on earth?

Was he to go out of the world branded with shame and ignominy? It was to be, and no earthly power could save him.

He sat in one of the topmost rooms of the old barracks. To-morrow he would be lying in his grave.

Bertram Wraydon went through his past life—his boyhood at Eton, where he had earned the name of Bertram the Swift-footed; he had carried all before him at the college sports; race after race on the flat and over hurdles had fallen to him, until it was impossible to handicap him out of any event.

He smiled as he thought of those days, but the smile died away quickly, and gave place to a shadow of deep pain.

Bertram went to the window and looked out. It was a dark night; rain fell in torrents, and the wind was moaning over the old town.

In a few hours all would be over. There was comfort in that. Whatever the world might think or say of him would not disturb his rest, but Helen, the sweetest and dearest girl, who loved him so, how could he think of her, alone and heartbroken?

The key clicked in the lock, the door opened, and the sergeant of the guard appeared.

"Mr. Philbrick," the man said, gruffly. "He has the colonel's permission to stay with you for half an hour."

Bertram Wraydon turned and faced the barrister who had defended him so ably.

Philbrick, a quick-eyed, fresh-coloured man, about thirty years of age, smiled as he held out his hand.

"Upon my word, I expected a better welcome, Lieutenant Wraydon," he said.

"Lieutenant! You mock me! I am only Bertram Wraydon. To-morrow I shall be nothing!"

"Well, well," said the barrister, seating himself at the table, "I am not here to quibble on such a matter. I came to ask if I can be of any assistance to you in a legal sense."

"I have nothing to leave. My half-brother, Hubert Sedgefield, will inherit all. Such was the provision of my father's will in the event of my death."

"Your half-brother, Hubert Sedgefield, is a lawyer?" Philbrick mused.

"Yes. I wish to forget him. He has not taken any hand in this matter," Bertram Wraydon replied.

"He has certainly not come forward to help you," Philbrick remarked.

"Why torture me? Why remind me of the agony I have undergone?"

"Because I believe you to be innocent—because, if I had the power, I would serve you. I have but this day arrived from London after petitioning the king in person, but George is hard to move. There is no hope, unless——"

He went to the door, and having made sure that neither the ear nor the eye of the sentry was at the keyhole, he continued: "Unless you can escape."

"Escape!" Bertram Wraydon repeated, hoarsely—"escape! How? Can I fly through walls of stone and brick, or leap forty feet to the ground? Would you have me commit suicide?"

"No, I would have you live, establish your innocence, and claim your fortune in the course of time," Philbrick replied, calmly. "On one side of this room lies the barrack-yard, on the other a road. There lies the way to liberty, forty feet down, as you say. Go to the window, and tell me what you see."

Bertram Wraydon obeyed, in a dull, mechanical sort of way. For the life of him he could not understand what Philbrick was driving at, and wished him gone.

"I see nothing likely to help me," he said.

"If a man can climb up the trunk of a tree, why should he not leap into the branches of one?"

Bertram Wraydon started, and the colour flew into his face. Now he knew what Philbrick meant.

Below grew a tall elm, and its branches were waving a few feet from the window.

"Ernest Philbrick," he said, "I might escape, for those arms seem to invite me to go to them. But what would follow? Would life be worth the having? How could I live, advertised for, hunted, a price set upon my head?"

"You have youth on your side," Philbrick replied. "You are also in the right. It is your duty to live to establish your innocence. Time flies. The sentry will soon be here, ordering me to be gone. Decide, and at once."

"I may be caught in the act of escaping," Wraydon said, half-dazed by the conflicting emotions surging through his brain.

"If so, you will have the consolation of knowing that you did your best to defeat your enemies. You have confided everything to me, as it was your duty to do. You have told me of your love for Helen Meadows——"

"Enough! I will make the attempt," Wraydon interrupted. "In any case, I can die but once."

"Spoken like a sensible man," said Philbrick. "If you succeed in reaching the foot of the tree, lift a big stone at the base of it, and underneath you will find a purse containing sufficient money for your present needs. Strike for the London Road, and speak to no man until one accosts you with his hat in his hand. He will say to you, 'The storm will pass away, I think.' Go with him; place your life in his hands, and he will not fail you."

"Heaven bless you! How can I ever repay you for this?" Wraydon said, grasping the barrister's hand.

"Fear not but that I shall present a bill of costs one of these days," said Philbrick. "But hark! The sentry returns. Wraydon," as the door opened, "good-bye. All shall know from me that you declare your innocence. You will not waver in that?"

"As Heaven is my witness, no!"

"Then should the evil moment come after all, die like a soldier and a man."

"Rest assured of that," said Wraydon. "Good-bye."

* * * * * *

Just before eight the roll of muffled drums was heard in the barrack-yard, but the sound did not fall on Bertram Wraydon's ears.

With slow and measured step the guard deputed to escort him to the final ordeal reached the room. The door was thrown open, but the officer looked in vain for the prisoner.

"Unhappy wretch!" he cried; "he has flung himself from the window and taken his own life!"

But there was nothing to tell that such was the case. The officer craned his neck out of the window, but saw no crushed or mangled body lying below.

"In the name of wonder," he cried, turning his white face to the men, "how did he manage it?"

Astounded, he rushed down the stairs, raising the alarm that Bertram Wraydon had escaped.

CHAPTER II.
At Wraydon House.—A Terrible Apparition.

WRAYDON HOUSE stood on the borders of Wraydon Wood. Eastwards it commanded a view of undulating arable and pasture land, of many hundred acres. Westwards, behind the wood, lay the village, and southward, the estate ran until it met with a winding river, and there the Wraydon estate, bringing in some thousands a year, ceased.

No Wraydon cantered on horseback in the park or rode to hounds now, for the last of the Wraydons had been declared by law to be dead, and Bertram Wraydon's half-brother, Hubert Sedgefield, was master of all.

The servants obeyed him, the tenants submitted to him, but all with ill grace. On the day that he took possession he made a flowery speech, but the people stood silent, eyeing him askance and doubtfully.

What had become of the real heir? Where was Bertram Wraydon, the handsome, generous lad, beloved by all?

There was not a man, woman, or child in the countryside that believed him guilty.

Young Wraydon a spy and traitor! They laughed the accusation to scorn, and flung it in Sedgefield's teeth, until his evil soul took arms against the humble folk.

He had tried soft words, and now he would see what persecution could do. The law was on his side, and he, a lawyer, knew how far he could go.

Farmers who came to renew leases were informed that better tenants could be found; the poor were sent empty-handed away; the servants were dismissed one by one, their places being filled by men and women of whom nothing was known.

Colonel Manfred often visited Wraydon House, and the people pointed to him and Hubert Sedgefield as they rode by, and whispered:

"There go the men who worked all the mischief, and robbed us of our young master."

One evening matters reached a climax, when a farmer, more outspoken than the rest, was sent for by Sedgefield.

He was received in a dark, shadowy room, in which Sedgefield and Colonel Manfred posed like a pair of judges at the head of a table.

"Gould," Sedgefield said, "I hear that you have been letting your tongue run loosely about me and my friend, Colonel Manfred. Such a state of things I cannot allow. If you were a rich man I could obtain damages from you, but as you are not, I can only order you to pay your rent, pack up, and go."

"And willingly, too," Gould replied. "My time's up in a month from to-day, and it was my intention to tell you that I didn't intend to turn a furrow again under such a landlord as you. We look upon you as a usurper and more, I tell you. There's not a man living twenty miles round but would give ten years of his life to know that Mr. Wraydon had got his own again. Ay, and they'd shelter and help him, too. If he came to me to-night I'd not turn him away, in spite of all the laws that were ever made, and all the grinding lawyers that ever brought misery on poor people."

"You hear that, colonel," said Sedgefield, turning his black eyes upon him; "this fellow makes no bones about the matter."

Colonel Manfred leaned back in his chair, and tugged at his grey moustache.

"Why pay attention to such a clod?" he said. "Let him go, and good riddance to him. How can the vapourings of a taproom harm you or me?"

"Clod!" echoed Gould. "Have a care, powerful as you may think yourself to be. Look out, or this fist of mine shall find its way between your eyes, and it has knocked down many a better man than you. Clod! If it means a simple man who pays his debts and looks the world in the face, I thank Heaven that I am a clod and not a thief, and plotting with a thief."

Hubert Sedgefield turned livid.

"Leave this house, you scoundrel!" he hissed. "My agent shall deal with you."

"A guilty man always gets angry when he hears the truth," Gould replied, turning on his heel. "Do your worst, and a fig for all you can do! I'll live to see Bertram Wraydon back again, and both of you hanged for conspiracy."

With this parting shot the sturdy farmer, flaming with rage, swung his brawny shoulders round and went downstairs, upsetting a bullet-headed footman on his way.

"Yes," Gould roared up the staircase, "and when the time comes, I'll walk a hundred miles if needs be on my bare feet to see you swung on a roadside gibbet."

"Death and Hades! this fellow shall sit in the stocks; I'll have him pelted to death in the pillory; he shall be arraigned at the next assizes——"

"Sit still, and keep your temper," said Colonel Manfred, gripping Sedgefield's arm, and forcing him back into his chair. "The more you blow the fire, the greater the flame."

"But if this is the sort of talk such men as he indulge in, my character will be ruined."

"Neither your character nor mine will suffer much," the colonel said. "Tush, man! Let them talk. All the talk in the world will not take a shilling out of your pocket—or mine. And that reminds me of the real object of my visit."

"Money, of course," said Hubert Sedgefield.

"Money, of course, and there is no reason for you to look so disagreeable about it. I have served you well."

"You charge heavily for your services," Sedgefield remarked, "but I do not grumble. An agreement is an agreement all the world over, so here is your fee, which makes us quits for six months."

He pushed a bundle of notes across the table, and the colonel thrust them into his pocket, saying:

"I will not take the trouble to count them, as I am in a hurry to depart."

"You are the last man in the world I should think of being on the wrong side of the ledger with," Sedgefield retorted, drawing his finger and thumb down his sallow cheeks. "When you are ready to go, I will see you as far as the door."

"And when there you need not be too profuse with your blessings," the colonel observed. Then, looking round the room, with a dark shadow in every corner, in spite of a dozen lighted candles, "Zounds, sir, I have no desire to stay here longer than I can possibly help. People always declared it to be haunted, but such a dry-as-dust lawyer as you, young though you be, is no doubt proof against ghosts."

Hubert Sedgefield gave the colonel an ugly sidelong look.

"Many a true word is spoken in jest," he said. "I have seen nothing; but I have heard enough to drive a nervous man out of any house. Only last night——"

"My horse is at the door; I can hear him champing impatiently at the bit," Colonel Manfred interrupted. "Come to my place in London and tell me all about it. Noises! Ha, ha! Fancy Hubert Sedgefield paying heed to noises in a house with more rooms in it than there are weeks in a year! Take a brace of pistols to bed with you, and take comfort in them. I'll guarantee to lay the finest ghost that ever frightened a silly old woman into fits, with a bullet."

By this time they had reached the door. The colonel stopped and looked into the night, as dark as pitch, and silent as the grave.

"I suppose my eyes will grow accustomed to this blackness," he said. "My horse is sure-footed and knows the way, or I might hesitate before riding across the heath."

"Why not stay?" Sedgefield demanded. "I have not dined yet. What is that you are muttering? Do you think I would poison you?"

Colonel Manfred laughed as he mounted into the saddle.

"My dear Sedgefield," he said, gathering the reins in his hands, "I fear you are growing fidgety and impetuous. Impetuosity leads to indiscretion, and the man who is indiscreet with his tongue is nothing more or less than a fool. Good-night! Take care of yourself. Come to me when you will, and rest assured that I will look well after you."

The horse went off at a foot pace, but it and its rider were soon lost to view in the density of the gloom.

Hubert Sedgefield stood at the open door. He had taken care that no servant should linger near it while he and the colonel exchanged the final words.

"But for one thing I would rid myself of him!" he hissed through his teeth. "He suspects me, and were he missed but an hour longer than the time he states, I should have his men clamouring at the door. A plague fall on them, one by one! I am in their hands, and my money alone stops their tongues. But wait! It is the diamond that cuts the diamond, and I must fight them with their own weapons. Phew! How hot it is! The sky will be ablaze with lightning soon."

The great hall was illumined by a chandelier holding a score and more wax candles, against which hung numbers of glass lustres to reflect the light in various colours. Above the hall ran two large galleries, with staircases leading to them, after the style of old houses.

The galleries were lighted with long windows, opening outwards, and two or three stood open now to admit the air.

Sedgefield's way lay under the gallery on the right-hand side, along a passage, and up a staircase leading to the library.

Locking the great door, and muttering a final curse on the head of Colonel Manfred, adding a hope that his horse might throw him and break his neck, Hubert Sedgefield retraced his footsteps.

They echoed so loudly and strangely on the marble floor that he stopped, half-believing that someone was following him.

"Fool!" he said, with a backward glance over his shoulder. "Fool!"

Then his heart seemed to stand still, his brain reeled, and he stood gaping and gasping for breath.

Round one of the windows a pair of eyes, set in a devilish face, were glaring at him. Shoulders, arms, body, and legs followed quickly, and the creature, leaping upon the gallery-rail, ran upon it with astonishing speed.

What it was, Sedgefield in his terror could not make out. The form was human, but it had the agility of an ape.

Man or fiend, it dropped into the hall, leaped upwards, spreading out what appeared to the horror-stricken spectator a pair of bat-like wings, and then flapped and wriggled on its hands and toes towards him like some uncouth monster, part man, part beast, part bird.

Men startled by apparitions, real or imaginary, have fallen dead, and left the story of their horror upon their faces. Life seemed to leave Hubert Sedgefield. A dreadful darkness grew before his eyes, he clutched at his heart with one hand, and groped blindly with the other along the wall until he collapsed and lay still.

An arm went round him and raised him to his feet. He opened his eyes, and saw one of his men-servants bending over him.

"What ails you, sir?" the man said. "Why did you call for help?"

"I call! Did I? I have no recollection." Then, as he remembered: "In the name of Heaven, what horror is this? Is it man or devil? Did you not see it? Keep it away from me!"

Another servant came tearing along the passage, and the two men looked at each other, and shook their heads.

Their master was going to be ill, they thought, and the sooner medical aid was summoned the better for him.

"We have seen nothing, sir," said one. "Look! The hall is empty, and as for the door, you shut it yourself."

"You saw nothing!" Sedgefield cried, with his hand clasping his clammy brow. "Nothing! Do I speak calmly, or like a madman? I tell you, I saw it—a gruesome thing—creep through yonder window. It had the face of Mephistopheles; it leaped and ran as no human ever leaped and ran. Hark! What is that?"

"Thunder!" replied one of the men.

"Order me a horse!" Sedgefield cried. "I must overtake Colonel Manfred. I cannot stay here. I should go mad. Why do you stand staring at me? Do my bidding, or take the consequences. A horse, I tell you! I'll not stay here, I tell you!"

"He'll have his way, though death comes of it," said one man to the other. "Ring the groom's bell twice, and he'll know that the squire requires his horse."

"My boots, hat, and riding-coat, quick!" yelled Sedgefield. "Curse you, why do you not move quicker than snails? Who is master here? You or I? Ah! my horse comes. Throw open the door, and tell me if you see aught in the way."

The lightning gleamed into the hall, and the thunder rolled again.

"There is nothing, sir," said the affrighted man. "The avenue is quite clear; but must you go, sir? Pray be persuaded——"

Hubert Sedgefield flung the man aside.

"Help me to get these things on," he said, as his hat, boots, and coat were brought him. "Now my whip and spurs. Hades! What an age it seems! Everything goes wrong! Ready at last! Hold the stirrup while I mount. Follow on, Fayer, follow on. The pace will not be so furious after I have overtaken the colonel."

"Not I," said Fayer. "I was not hired to ride with a madman through a thunderstorm. And mad he is beyond a doubt. Did you ever see the like of him, Bill Robson?"

Bill Robson, the groom, took his chin between his fingers, and gave it a twist.

"No," he replied—"no; and I'm not likely to make a fortune in his service. A bad man is always a haunted man, so they say. Whew! There's a flash, and now for the crash! Sane or mad, let him ride on. I suppose his complaint is in trying to see how soon he can empty the wine-cellar."

"No," Fayer replied. "It isn't that. The squire's not a hard-drinking man, but he's got something on his mind. Hollick, go and shut those windows, or the place will be swamped soon."

"If you think I'm going up there alone, you take me for an idiot," Hollick said.

"All three of us had better go, then," Fayer said. "Bill Robson, come below stairs, and keep us company. We'll see no more of him until he gets over this scare."

"Take my advice, and don't go frightening the feymales about what the squire thought he saw," Robson said. "I tell you he's been drinking, and if he isn't found in a ditch, it will be a wonder to me."

Meanwhile, Hubert Sedgefield had galloped down the avenue and through the village, hot in pursuit of Colonel Manfred.

Soon the colonel heard him coming, and suspecting an attack from a highwayman, drew a pistol from his pocket, and wheeled his horse round.

A glare of lightning revealed his pursuer, and the colonel uttered a cry of astonishment.

"What brings you here?" he demanded. "Pull up, man! Pull up, or you'll ride over me! Sedgefield, keep your distance! If you have come for mischief, I am prepared to meet it. I have a pistol here, and will send a bullet through your brain if you attempt to do me harm!"

"Mischief!—I mean no mischief," Sedgefield replied, swaying unsteadily in the saddle. "I want your company and your help. I have received a visit from a devil."

The lightning flashed again, and the thunder crashed in the sky.

"Bah!" said the colonel, as Sedgefield rode to his side. "Your mind is full of fancies. I noticed that you looked ill at ease, but I did not think you would play the part of a child. But ride with me if you will."

The storm was rolling up, increasing in force every moment.

"I will sell Wraydon House," Sedgefield said, as they set spurs to their horses again. "I dare not return to the place. It is accursed and haunted by such a form as mortal eyes never yet gazed upon. I saw it, I tell you, and, Manfred, it——"

Just then the lightning blazed and the thunder crashed in such an awful manner that the horses reared and snorted in affright.

"We'll have no more gruesome stories, or Broxbourne won't see us to-night. We'll put up at the 'Rosebush' Inn. By Pluto! the heavens seem on fire. Push on your nag, Sedgefield."

As the thunder rolled muttering away, there came into the air another sound that filled the souls of the two men with terror.

It was a peal of mocking laughter, and the colonel, looking back, beheld a figure approaching by terrific leaps.

"Look!" he yelled. "Sedgefield, do you not see?"

"It is the same figure that I saw. Powers of mercy, it is following us!"

The uncanny figure became visible and invisible by turns. It was that of a man wearing a tight-fitting tunic, slashed in front with white, as though his ribs were laid bare. But whoever dreamed of a man taking such leaps, or looked upon such eyes as gleamed from the demoniacal head, upon which sat a tight-fitting cap surmounted with a feather.

If man it was, he seemed to be gifted with the power of flying, for no sooner did his feet touch the earth than he rose in the air, and with bound on bound sped onward like a panther.

"Ha, ha, ha!" screamed the creature. "The hour of retribution will come! Unholy wretches and perjurers, thieves and villains, the earth shall not hide you from me! An eye for an eye, and a tooth for a tooth!"

Colonel Manfred fired a pistol at the awful figure, as lightning blue and red played upon it, and flung the weapon from him when another burst of maddening laughter greeted his ears.

"On! on!" he shrieked. "We have no man to deal with!"

Then whip and spur, spur and whip. The terrified men lashed and goaded their horses as they looked back, until the tortured animals seemed to fly over the ground.

On, and still on, now with the roaring of the thunder, and now the peals of mocking laughter in their ears.

On and on, dazed and half-blinded by the lightning and the rush and rattle of the deluge of rain and hail falling about them.

Again, with faces livid with the very agony of terror, they looked back.

Oh, the horror of it! The figure seemed to be gaining upon them. There seemed to be no escape. A few more mighty bounds and the man, or fiend, would pounce upon them, but the "Rosebush" Inn was at hand.

The door stood open, and an orange glow of light fell upon the road.

Then hostelry and everything vanished in one mighty flare as the heavens opened, and a fire-ball, hurtling from the sky, burst into a very furnace of flame.

What followed the men scarcely knew. Bewildered, deafened by the explosion that followed as the fire-ball struck the earth, they flung themselves out of the saddle, and letting their horses go, staggered into the hostelry.

The lower rooms were full of people who had taken shelter from the storm. The landlord, his wife, servants, constable, beadle, tradesmen, farmers, drovers, travellers were all huddled together.

Never had they witnessed such a scene, and all thought that the world had come to an end.

Wild, distraught, and ghastly, Colonel Manfred and Hubert Sedgefield rushed into their midst.

"The Evil One is abroad!" the colonel gasped. "We have seen him riding on the wings of the storm. Landlord! Where is the landlord? Give me some brandy, or I shall die!"

The landlord, Peter Bloggs, looked as if he stood in need of some strong stimulant himself. His face was a lovely green, and big and burly as he was he shook all over like a jelly.

"I'd not go into the bar among them bright things for a thousand pounds!" he said, stammering in his speech.

"Oh, it's you, Colonel Manfred, and you, Squire. You are so changed that I did not recognise you at first. Heaven preserve us! what a night!"

"The storm is dying away," someone said. "Let us be thankful that we find ourselves alive. We shall hear of some dreadful damage being done."

At that moment the wind blew the door to with a loud bang, and the constable fell into the arms of the beadle, who having quite enough to do to support his own tottering limbs, hit the guardian of the public peace below the belt, and doubled him up on the floor.

No notice was taken of the assault, nor of the constable's outcry that the end of his earthly career had come.

The lightning was still blazing on the blinds, and through every chink and cranny, the thunder was still rolling, but the storm was abating, and suddenly the rain ceased, and the worst was over.

The landlady removed her apron from her head; the female domestics took their fingers from their ears; the guests brightened up, and a waiter, with smudges on his face suggesting that he had not been far away from the coal-cellar, came in, and seeing Colonel Manfred and Hubert Sedgefield, offered to escort them to a private room.

They went with him willingly enough, and presently Peter Bloggs, now smiling and inclined to be festive, followed, and took their orders.

Between gulps of brandy they told their story, and Peter sank into a chair.

"A fiend—a storm fiend, that's what it was," he said. "We live in awful times, gentlemen. Bill, bring me some brandy, and don't pour it outside the glass. Oh, lor! what will the people say? Here's a pretty tale for the country-folk. Leaped as high as your heads when you were on horseback? Murder! We're all lost! Where's Joe Braid, the beadle? Tell him to send for the parson."

Just then a man, battered by the wind and drenched to the skin, drove up to the door.

"Is there no ostler attached to this accursed house?" he cried. "House! house! Has the fiend I saw just now flown away with you all?"

Leaping from a cart, he rushed into the house.

"I've seen such a sight as man never saw before," he cried. "As I was driving over the bridge that crosses the river something leaped clean over me and vanished into Blue Bell Copse."

He staggered into a chair, and moaned hysterically as the people gathered round him.

"Vanished into Blue Bell Copse," said the constable, forgetting how severely he had been smitten; "my house is at the end of it. Don't come here with such a yarn. It's a lie to frighten me."

"It ain't a lie," the landlord cried, running in. "Colonel Manfred and Squire Sedgefield saw it, too. The foul fiend's got loose among us."

At this there were gasps, groans, and screams.

"Let's all go and see if we can make anything of it," said the constable, taking a thick staff, and flourishing it viciously at the beadle. "I'll make one."

"It's your dooty to look into the matter yourself," observed a farmer. "Landlord, keep a bed for me; I'll stay here to-night."

"What about your wife, Jem Dickers?" demanded a man, shivering in a corner. "Won't she be alarmed at your absence?"

"I like a man who minds his own business," Jem Dickers retorted. "I've got business to do at Bishop Stortford to-morrow, so here I stay."

"I call for volunteers," said the constable. "I call upon you all in the name of the king! Bloggs, load your blunderbuss, and come along!"

"I'll see your neck as long as my arm first," Peter Bloggs replied, emphatically. "I don't mind having a fair stand-up fight with a man, but when it comes to a thing that's a man but isn't a man, and can fly like a bat, I'd rayther be excused."

"That means that you'll leave me to go home alone," said the constable. "Oh, you precious set of cowards!"

It so happened, however, that the homeward journey of several others lay in the direction of Blue Bell Copse, and as Peter Bloggs announced that all the beds were taken and the house could not be added to on so short a notice, several brave and valiant men laid their heads together.

At length it was decided to borrow the landlord's blunderbuss, two stable-lanterns, as many pitchforks, and a rusty pistol used for scaring crows.

The blunderbuss was entrusted to Josiah Legge, a lanky farmer, the best shot in the neighbourhood, and he took front rank with the constable, who, with a lantern in one hand and his staff of office in the other, called upon the others to keep close.

"Keep your eyes on me," he said. "If I start running one way, don't you run the other."

Someone laughed, and the constable cast a wrathful eye over his shoulder.

"What I meant to say," he growled, "that if I run after this—this—I hardly know what to call it—don't you wheel about and leave me in the lurch. Legge, would you mind holding the blunderbuss in front of you instead of pointing it at my nose?"

"I don't want any man here to tell me how to handle fire-arms," Josiah Legge replied, angrily. "I've used 'em almost since I could walk."

"Fire-irons!" cried a voice.

"Who said that?" demanded Legge, stopping, as the black fringe of the copse came into view. "You, Sam Bullifant, constable of the parish, what are you getting behind me for?"

"I want to find out who is making game of us," Bullifant replied. "If I do find out, that man's head won't be free of aching this time to-morrow night. But," he added, with a puzzled look on his face, "the voice seemed to come from the air!"

All traces of the storm, save of a faint quivering on the horizon, were gone, and the stars were shining brightly in a deep indigo-blue sky, but there was no moon, and the lanterns gave an uncertain and weird kind of light.

"I do hope," said Josiah Legge, shouldering

the blunderbuss and keeping his finger on the trigger—"I do hope that we are friends and neighbours, and that there is no man among us unkind enough to make rude remarks at another at such a time as this. Bullifant, you come forward!"

"A stone has worked its way into my boot," the constable said. "Gone right through the sole into my big toe."

"It seems to me that we've got a coward as well as a fool among us," Legge said. "Hallo! What's that up there? Ah-h-h-h!"

He pointed to a tree, and out of the branches was peering a face, a pale-yellow light playing about it.

The horrified spectators had just time to note a pointed moustache and eyebrows, large, brightly-glaring eyes and grinning mouth, when Josiah Legge's finger tightened on the trigger, and the blunderbuss exploded with a report that awoke the echoes far and wide.

The charge cut a pitchfork in two, blew off a man's hat, and in a moment a stampede took place.

"Ha, ha, ha!" yelled a voice. "I'll come down! Wait for me, ye dogs! Wait, and learn that to meet with Spring-heeled Jack means death!"

It seemed that the stone had slipped out of the constable's boot as easily as it had slipped in, for he started off at an amazing rate, with Joe Braid clinging to his coat-tails.

As they reached the bridge—and there the road was narrow—the crush was terrific, and Legge, feeling that he was being slowly squeezed over the parapet, seized the beadle's ears and hung on to them with an amount of energy quite worthy of the cause.

The mocking laughter followed them as they ran, and seemed to be always close to them.

On they went, without blunderbuss, lanterns, staves, or clubs, helter-skelter, and anyhow.

Peter Bloggs did not expect another visit from the men who had set out so valiantly, and he was considerably astonished when Sam Bullifant, who had never lost first place, plunged in, and butted him just where he tied his apron-strings.

It seemed to Bloggs that, having gone through the wall into the next room, he turned several somersaults before he alighted on his back. He had hardly become conscious that his wife was attacking the constable, and that the room was full of men roaring and shouting themselves hoarse, when someone cried out that Joe Braid, the beadle, had mistaken the kitchen-fire for a chair, and was roasting himself to death.

"The parish will pay for 'em," Braid said, alluding to his breeches, after he had been rescued. "Oh, Bloggs—oh, Mr. Bloggs, we shall all be murdered in our beds or carried away in red fire. We've seen him! Oh, pray, do listen! We've seen the fiend!"

They all swore to it, they swore to having seen the dreadful form, and heard it, too, and Peter Bloggs sat in a corner listening, with his eyes working to and fro like a clockwork figure.

"If so be I'm going to die through a darned constable, amen," he said.

"Get up and tell me what I am to do," his wife cried. "These people say that they will not go home."

"Well, let 'em stay," Bloggs mumbled. "Who cares? I'll be dead afore the morning. Where's Bullifant? I want to say a few words to him wery close."

But Bullifant, wise in his generation, held aloof. So the landlord got up, edged sideways into the bar, and came forth looking better.

And all night long the story was told and retold, but when dawn came the men slunk away, with "Spring-heeled Jack" still lingering on their lips.

CHAPTER III.

A Scene in Court. — Ernest Philbrick Receives a Visit.—On the Track of the Fugitive.

THE Ipswich summer assizes were in progress. The evil-smelling court was packed from floor to ceiling. With bouquets of flowers on each side, and sweet-smelling herbs strewn in front, the old judge sat dozing over his notebook.

The jury, however, were on the alert, and turned their eyes on the prisoner in the dock, a young, poorly-clad man.

His advocate was making a passionate appeal on his behalf, and the whole court was hanging on to his words. But the judge dozed on. He was used to the flowery words of counsel.

"Gentlemen," cried the barrister, Ernest Philbrick by name—"gentlemen, a man's life is in your hands. I implore you, as each and every one of you will one day appear before a higher tribunal, to ponder well on the verdict you will give. It means life or death.

"Gentlemen, I will present two pictures before you. The first is a bright one. This man will return to his wife and two little children. His wife will greet him with wild delight; his children will climb to his knee and kiss the face so long a stranger to them."

Here the judge became conscious that he was snoring, sat up, and, bending over his notebook, scratched something in a corner, with a noisy pen.

"The second picture, gentlemen," continued Ernest Philbrick, "is as dark as the other is bright. If you say that this man is guilty, he will leave the dock a doomed man. Nothing will then save him from a felon's death. He is, as you know, accused of robbery on the highway, and yet, even according to the evidence of the prosecution, to commit such a crime he must have run at the astonishing rate of two miles in nine minutes. Look at him! There he stands in the same boots and clothes that he wore when arrested. Gentlemen, you will say with me that such a feat is impossible. The prosecution might as well have declared my client to be Spring-heeled Jack."

"One moment," said the judge. "You have made an allusion to Spring-heeled Jack. Last evening's 'Post' made some wild reference to him. Who is he and what is he?"

"That, my lord, is a mystery," Philbrick replied. "It appears that he possesses such wonderful powers that people do not believe him to be mortal. It is said that he can clear an obstacle twelve feet in height."

The judge laughed softly.

"It is wonderful what foolish people can be made to believe," he said. "Spring-heeled Jack, indeed. It is time that his heels were cooling on the floor of some gaol. But go on with your address. I am sorry that I interrupted you. Spring-heeled Jack, indeed! Ha, ha!"

"You have put his lordship in a good temper and won your case," a barrister whispered in Philbrick's ear.

And so it happened, for the judge took the same view as the defence, and the prisoner was acquitted.

When, with a glad cry, he had run out of court, the judge said:

"It is time that the court is adjourned, but before we go, I should like to know if anyone knows more about Spring-heeled Jack than has appeared in print?"

An officer stood up.

"My lord," he said, "a number of people are willing to take their oaths that they have seen him. He appears in different parts of the country with a rapidity that is astounding. What his object is has not yet transpired, but, as the learned barrister here said, the people do not believe him to be mortal, but the spirit of one who, in his lifetime, did some fearful crime."

"A most troublesome ghost, certainly," his lordship observed. "I should think that a brace of good pistols with bullets in them would stop his jumping. The court stands adjourned until to-morrow at ten o'clock."

Ernest Philbrick packed his briefs in a bag, and handing it to his clerk, an exceedingly sharp youth, left the court in the company of several other barristers.

His rooms were at the "Great White Horse" Hotel, and no sooner had he dined and rested an hour, than he was at work again, poring over briefs, and turning the leaves of books, dry enough to make a man thirsty.

At the other end of the table sat his clerk, as stiff as a poker, and as dumb as a drum with a hole in it.

His name was Jerry Slye, and he had picked up so much law that he often made himself useful to the successful barrister.

"Jerry," said Ernest Philbrick, suddenly, leaning back in his chair, and clasping his hands behind his head, "what do you think of these stories about Spring-heeled Jack?"

"I think that, if he can jump so high, he might go to a better place than where people say he comes from," Jerry replied.

"My young friend, you seem to have been dining on needles and pins," Philbrick said. "Of course you and the other clerks have been talking about this mysterious creature, so I thought that your opinion might be worth having."

"My opinion is that he's what the people put him down to be—a demon. As to dining, I haven't tasted food since breakfast. You see, sir, you have been so busy."

"My poor lad, go at once and get some dinner, and spend the rest of the evening where you like," said Philbrick.

Jerry Slye stood up, and, rattling some money in his pocket, put his head on one side, and, closing one eye, gazed wistfully at the barrister with the other.

"What is the matter with you?" Philbrick demanded. "Why do you look at me like that, and why do you not go and save yourself from starvation?"

"I've been waiting to speak to you," Jerry replied. "As I was coming along with the brief-bag, a man tapped me on the shoulder and put two guineas into my hand."

"Very good of him," the barrister observed.

"Just what I thought," said Jerry Slye. "He was paying at a high rate, considering that all he wanted of me was to know what part of the hotel he could find you."

"And you told him?"

Jerry Slye nodded his head, and rattled his money again.

"You should have consulted me first," Philbrick said. "The man may have some supposed grievance against me. He may be a madman with an imaginary wrong in his mind and a pistol in his pocket."

"You didn't think that I opened my mouth until I made sure of him," Jerry responded. "Not I, oh, dear, no! The man said to me: 'I want to see Mr. Philbrick, because he did me the greatest service that any man can do for another. He saved my life, and I want to express my gratitude to him in person.'"

"This sounds rather mysterious," the barrister said, with a pensive look in his eyes. "Is that all?"

"Not quite, sir. The man gave me this, and said that if you put your memory to the test, you might remember it," and Jerry Slye held out a ring.

Ernest Philbrick took the ring, and, having examined it thoroughly, put it on his own finger.

"Why did you not give me this before?" he demanded.

"Because the man told me to keep it until eight o'clock, and it's just on the strike now."

"Well," said the barrister, "I suppose I must not be angry with you. I seem to recognise this ring, although I may be mistaken, but I will see the man, as he seems to be harmless. Now, run away to your dinner."

Jerry Slye was scarcely on the other side of the door, when the barrister rose and began to pace the room. He knitted his brow, and a troubled look spread over his face.

"He might have chosen some more distant part of the country," he said. "Here he was as well known as any man in the neighbourhood. Rash! rash! I must get him away as soon as possible, or trouble will come of it. Ha!"

The door had opened, and a tall man, wearing a long cloak, was standing in the room.

"Bertram Wraydon," Philbrick said, "you here! Lock the door, or one of the waiters may come in. I hope for your sake that no one saw you enter the hotel."

"I did not come in at the front door, or at any door at all," Wraydon replied, dropping the cloak at his feet.

"Then in the name of wonder how did you get here?" Philbrick demanded. "Why, hang it! that is my cloak you have just flung off!"

"I borrowed it from the stand on the landing," Wraydon replied, coolly. "You ask me how I got here. I suppose it is reasonable to assume that a man who can jump out of a window and reach the ground with safety can jump in at one?"

"I—I do not quite understand," the barrister said, putting his hand to his brow. "I only know that you are here at the risk of your life. Wraydon, I thought that you went abroad."

"So I did, but I returned some time ago, and I am here to refund what I owe you."

"Hang what you owe me!" Philbrick blurted out. "If you are discovered, there will be joy in the camp of your enemies, and it will not be a shooting business this time."

"I recognise that," Wraydon replied. "Catching spells hanging to me, but I am pretty confident that I can make that a difficult matter. Here is the money you lent me, and here with my hand on my heart I thank you."

"Sit down!" Philbrick said. "Now you have come, I want to know how you have fared; but what is this you are paying me in? Some of these coins are as old as Charles I. They are in a splendid state of preservation. Where in the name of wonder did you chance upon them?"

"To tell you how I became possessed of them would make a longer story than you might be inclined to listen to," Wraydon replied. "You will remember that, while you were preparing my defence, I told you that I had some clue of treasure buried beneath Wraydon House during the Civil War? Well, I followed up the clue, and unearthed the treasure."

"Are you mad or am I dreaming?" Philbrick cried. "You have been to Wraydon House to make the rope that will hang you, I suppose? But how pale and hollow-eyed you are, Wraydon! Pray drink some wine, and get some colour into your face."

"Thank you," Wraydon said, helping himself. "No, Philbrick, I have not turned Wraydon House into a rope-walk for the benefit of the hangman. I went there for other purposes than to secure the treasure; my other object was to see Colonel Manfred and my half-brother, Hubert Sedgefield; and I have seen them."

"You have seen them!" Philbrick walked to the hearth, and leaned heavily against the mantelshelf. "That means they must have seen you; if so, my rash young friend, all the fat is in the fire, and beyond a doubt there is a pretty pack of hounds on your track. They'll be giving tongue soon."

"You are wrong," Wraydon said; "they did not see me, although at one time I was almost as close to them as I am to you."

"Wraydon," said Ernest Philbrick, "talk like a rational man. Explain your meaning, and, having done so, take my advice and get back to the Continent. If you have money, you can enjoy yourself there, and there bide your time. Believe me that I have still your case in hand, and will leave no stone unturned to bring about a happy result. As for yourself, you can do nothing. You tell me that you have been to Wraydon House, that you have unearthed treasure, and that you have seen Colonel Manfred, Hubert Sedgefield, and others who brought about your downfall, and that they have seen you, and yet not recognised you."

"All true, I assure you."

"I am a plain man, and it is my business to deal with plain facts," Philbrick said. "In the name of all that is wonderful, I ask you to tell me——"

At that moment someone tried the door, and then knocked sharply at it.

"Who is there?" demanded Philbrick, starting across the room.

"Jerry Slye," came the reply through the keyhole.

"What do you want?"

"Two strange men have been inquiring for you, and they are coming upstairs."

"This is a most awkward dilemma," the barrister whispered, turning to Wraydon. "Step behind the curtain while I speak to these men; I will get rid of them in a minute or two."

The curtains concealing the window hung in long, thick folds, and Wraydon disappeared behind them.

Whistling and humming a tune, Ernest Philbrick unlocked the door, opened it, and walked on the landing, as if it were his intention to descend the stairs.

He was met by two men. One he knew only too well, the other was a stranger to him; but Philbrick was too keen of eye not to detect an officer in private clothes.

"Mr. Sedgefield," he cried, "this is a surprise. Of all men in the world you are the last I thought of seeing."

"The unexpected always happens, or nearly so," Hubert Sedgefield said. "I was in court to-day when you got that fellow off. He was guilty, of course, and must think himself lucky in being able to secure so talented an advocate."

"Compliments do not sit upon me like a well-fitting coat," Philbrick returned, coldly. "Mr. Sedgefield, I am both tired and busy. To what cause may I attribute the honour of your visit?"

"Most important business, I assure you.

It refers to a cause you took most absorbing interest in, but were not quite so lucky."

"You refer to your half-brother, Bertram Wraydon?"

"Exactly," replied Sedgefield.

"I can give you only a minute," Philbrick said. "This is not my consulting room proper; there is one downstairs——"

"It will do just as well," Sedgefield interrupted.

"As you like," the barrister said, with a choking feeling in his throat, but keeping outwardly calm. "Who is your friend?"

"Mr. Jonas Hitchman."

"How do you do, Mr. Hitchman?" said Philbrick, waving his hand towards two chairs and devoutly wishing that his visitors were at the bottom of the sea. "Now, Mr. Sedgefield, state your business, and pray remember that I have no time to spare. Look at that pile of briefs; they must be read and thought over before the court assembles to-morrow."

"Briefly, then," said Sedgefield, chuckling at his own joke, "Bertram Wraydon has been seen in England, in this very county, and on this very day."

"You astonish me!" said Ernest Philbrick.

"Knowing how friendly disposed you were towards him, I thought it probable that he might have written to you, or called upon you," Sedgefield continued. "I'll not beat about the bush, Philbrick, but tell you that if you know anything about the scoundrel you had better out with it at once. If you conceal him, or aid and abet him in any way, the high position you hold in your profession will not save you. Mr. Hitchman, I may as well explain, is—er—in a manner of speaking, connected with the law."

There was nothing to be done but to take the bull by the horns, as the saying goes, and the barrister lost no time in doing so.

"I have listened to some impertinence in my time, but this caps all," he said. "I have only one answer to give you, Mr. Hubert Sedgefield, and that is—if you don't take yourself and this man out of the room immediately, you will compel me to have recourse to measures I should regret. It appears to me that you have been dining well but not wisely, or you would never dream of coming on such an audacious errand."

"That means I have been drinking," Hitchman said, smacking his lips, as if moisture of any kind, except tea, coffee, or water, would be welcome. "Just you mind what you say, or you'll find a writ in your pocket."

"Out of the room, you insolent scoundrel!" cried Philbrick.

"All right; I'm going," said Hitchman, backing slowly towards the door. "There's no occasion for violence. I'm a peaceable sort of man except when I've got a rough customer to handle, and then I go to any lengths. Mr. Sedgefield, you'd better come away."

"If he does not, I'll pitch him head-and-heels over the balustrade," Ernest Philbrick thundered. "You threaten me, do you? Why, you mean-spirited, contemptible rascal, wearing the coat and spending the money that belongs to another man, if it were not for the disgrace to touch you, I'd twist your nose out of shape!"

"You hear that, Hitchman?" Sedgefield said, skipping round the table. "This is the great Ernest Philbrick, who earns his living by defending spies, murderers, and pickpockets! Ha, ha, ha! We know what we suspect, my fine fellow, and we will keep our eyes on you!"

With that, Sedgefield made a run for the stairs, and went down them in double-quick time, with Hitchman following at his heels.

"Phew! what a near thing!" Philbrick muttered. "As for myself, I could have explained matters, but Wraydon would have been dished. Wraydon," he added, "you may come out."

There was no reply, and the thick plush curtain hung motionless, with a deep shadow in each fold.

"I repeat that you may come out," Philbrick said, shutting the door. "I'll have to smuggle you into my bedroom and put up with a couch. Come out, I say!"

Still no reply, and Ernest Philbrick began to lose patience.

"Confound the fellow!" he said. "I really believe that his troubles have driven him mad. What is the meaning of this extraordinary conduct?" pulling the curtains apart. "Wraydon, I'll have you to know—— Great Heaven! what has become of the man?"

Bertram Wraydon had vanished; melted, as it were, into thin air, leaving neither sign nor trace behind him.

The window was unlatched, but it was closed, as Philbrick himself had left it. On coming in, he had found it open, with a strong draught blowing in, and had shut it, for the reason that he had come hot and excited from a crowded court and had feared catching cold.

If he had been amazed at Wraydon's coming, he was a thousand times more so at his disappearance.

His blood chilled, and then surged through his veins like liquid fire. Was Bertram Wraydon dead, and had his spirit visited him? "There are more things in heaven and earth than are dreamt of in our philosophy."

But the thought was absurd. The money Wraydon had paid him was in his pocket, and ghosts do not pay in hard cash.

Laughing mirthlessly at his own folly, Ernest Philbrick pushed the window open and looked out.

The stable-yard lay below, and a man was busy grooming a horse. He looked up on hearing the window-frame creak on its hinges, and knuckled his forehead after the time-honoured fashion of ostlers.

"Whose horse is that?" the barrister asked.

"The master's," the ostler replied—"one of the changes for the Stowmarket Fly, and she'll be here in less than ten minutes. Whoa! stand still, you fifteen-mile-an-hourer. You won't be as frisky when you take a pull at the hill at the end of the stage."

"I thought I heard something like a man

falling," remarked Philbrick, scarcely knowing what to say.

"That was my mate, Ben Bolderry," the ostler said. "He's that ork'ard on his feet that he often tumbles over his own shadder."

"I see! I must have been mistaken. By the way, what is the height of that gate? I see it is closed."

"And locked, too," the ostler replied. "It's ten feet high, leaving out six inches of iron spikes on top. You'll excuse me, sir, but I must get on with my work, or there'll be Old Nick to pay if the 'osses ain't ready when the Stowmarket Fly comes up like a gale o' wind in—a wiolent hurry. She don't stop for no one, the Stowmarket Fly don't. She's the quickest thing on wheels as ever rolled along a road, she is!"

Ernest Philbrick shut the window and went back to his easy-chair at the table, and as he seated himself, but not without an uneasy glance over his shoulder, Jerry Slye walked into the room.

"So they are gone," he said, looking round. "I thought I had better tell you that they were asking for you."

"Quite right, Jerry—quite right," Philbrick replied. "But what about your dinner?"

"I've had a snack, sir; but, to tell the truth, my appetite wasn't nearly so good as usual. I suppose I must put it down to the weather, and I—I've got a bit of a headache, and so I thought I'd come back and see if you could find me something to do to keep me awake until bedtime."

The barrister bent his searching eyes on the lad's face, and saw that it was drawn and white.

"Jerry," he said, "you've either been up to some mischief or seen something to frighten you. Which is it? Tell me the truth, as I know you will, because I have never bowled you out in a lie."

"I'll tell you, if you are quite sure that no one is listening," Jerry replied, shuddering, and turning whiter still. "Would you mind looking behind the curtains and making certain that the window is fastened?"

"I can vouch for both, as I have just returned from the window."

"Well, then, sir," Jerry said, putting his hands to his face to stop the twitching of the muscles, "I've seen Spring-heeled Jack! Don't think I'm crazy, sir. I saw him—on the roof—and taking a flying leap from one chimney-stack to another, and then he went out of my sight just like a puff of smoke!"

"Have you spoken of this to anyone but me?" Philbrick demanded.

"No, sir," Jerry Slye replied. "To tell you the truth, I have not had much breath to speak with until I got back."

"Then keep your own counsel, or people will laugh at you."

"Perhaps you have seen Spring-heeled Jack yourself?" Jerry remarked.

"Seen Spring-heeled Jack! What should put such a thing into your head?"

"I don't know," Jerry replied, with a bewildered look in his eyes; "but things do seem a bit funny all round. I wish I could go to sleep, wake up, and forget all about it."

"Try the experiment by going to bed now," Ernest Philbrick remarked.

"How am I to know that Spring-heeled Jack won't drop down the chimney and frighten the life out of me?" Jerry's eyes grew rounder and rounder as he spoke, and he breathed so hard that some papers lying near him fluttered.

"Don't worry! Most likely he is flying at higher game," said the barrister. "We'll say no more about him. I want to get on with my work."

At that moment there came a clatter and the sound of many voices from the street.

"What's that?" cried Jerry, starting from his chair, with his hair on end.

"Only the coach called the Stowmarket Fly, you ninny!" Philbrick said. "Go down and see what is going on."

There was a goodly company below, as Jerry soon discovered. The coach was packed, mostly with well-to-do people, for only those with plenty of money could afford to travel by such an expensive conveyance.

Outside there were stout old gentlemen, and from the windows looked pretty faces, framed in wonderful bonnets.

The coachman had a face as wide as a warming-pan, and as ruddy as a harvest-moon in a mist. He wore a coat that came down to his heels, and a broad-brimmed hat round which a couple of rabbits might have run a race.

The guard, horn in hand, swung himself out of his perch, on which he balanced himself with the skill of a practised acrobat, when the coach swung round corners.

"No getting out here, ladies and gents," he said. "Only three minutes to stay, but if any gent feels thirsty, why, here's the landlord, and here's the waiters."

The tired horses were taken out, and the four fresh ones were being put in with astounding rapidity, when the coachman said, catching the reins on the whip-stalk, and sliding them into his left hand:

"What was Tom Claxton saying to you when we pulled up at Bentley?"

"He asked me if Spring-heeled Jack had given us a turn yet."

"If I'd been in your place, I'd have given Tom Claxton such a turn with my fist on his nose that 'u'd have made him do a little springin' hisself," the coachman growled. "It's all a lie—a darned lie, that's what it is! Fancy a man able to walk over 'ouses, and skip over churches with the same ease that a hoss nips over a mole-hill."

"Where do such reports come from?" one of the passengers asked, leaning forward.

"From the imaginations of a pack of fools," the coachman replied. "Now then! Ready there! Steady, my beauties! Ah! would you?" to one of the wheelers. "Mind what you are about, you naughty boy, or I'll tell your mother."

With a rattle and sparks flying from the cobble-stones, the coach whirled away.

Jerry Slye stood almost unnoticed among the crowd of loiterers and ostlers, and was so wrapped in his thoughts that a man prodded him three times in the ribs before the youth deigned to notice him.

"If you have a few minutes to spare," the man said, softly, in his ear, "I can show you the way to employ them to your advantage."

"That's about my style," Jerry replied, cheerfully. "We legal gents are always on the lookout for a good thing, and don't turn up our noses at a small one."

"Come with me, then," said the stranger, rustling a Bank of England note by way of impressing the lad.

"I'll go just a hundred yards down the road, but no further," Jerry said.

"But your master may see you."

The Bank of England note rustled louder.

"Oh, no, he won't," Jerry said. "He's upstairs reading his briefs."

"Very good," said the man. "I'll walk on, and you follow."

Jerry counted a hundred steps and stopped at the mouth of a dark and narrow entry.

"Now then, sir," he said, "what have you to say to me?"

"To ask you a question or two, and to pay well for them. You are Mr. Philbrick's clerk, and, of course, he sees a good many people?"

"Heaps! All sorts, all sizes, and all conditions," Jerry replied. "We have people who get into trouble through no fault of their own, and people who ought to be hanged for getting others into trouble."

"Does a gentleman named Wraydon ever come to see him?" the stranger whispered, slipping the note into Jerry's hand.

Jerry Slye returned the note, and walked backwards into the middle of the road.

"I don't know anything about Mr. Wraydon," he said; "but I know what you are driving at, and what you would have me do. You want me to take a paltry bribe to divulge my master's business. You don't know me. Put your dirty money in your pocket, and keep it for some scoundrel as bad as yourself. And mark this: I'll remember your face all my life."

Jerry saw the glint of steel flash from the man's sleeve.

"You mean murder, do you?" Jerry cried.

"What's up here?" demanded a man, coming out of the passage.

"Nothing," Jerry replied, as a thought flashed into his brain. "This gentleman's been asking me to take a note, but I'm too busy."

The tempter walked away, quickening the pace as he went.

Jerry followed him with his eyes until he disappeared, and then retraced his footsteps to the "Great White Horse."

"Bed's the best place for me," he said. "I'll say nothing about this to Mr. Philbrick now. I'll work this out in my own way."

CHAPTER IV
Tells of a Great Sensation.

MEANWHILE, the Stowmarket Fly was making excellent progress. The lamps gave forth a genial light, the coachman flicked the willing horses playfully, and the guard, a well-known character, being asked to sing, leaned back in the "dicky," and opening his mouth, roared:

"Old England, my Britons, would, but for the Tories,
　Be merry and happy and perfectly free ;
The flat flag of freedom—that emblem of glories—
　Would wave but for them o'er the land and the sea.
Her men are so brave, generous, joyous, and witty,
　It's seldom indeed you'll discover a rogue,
While the girls are so precious, plump, prattling,
　　and pretty,
　It's wonderful bigamy's not more in vogue.
　　Tol-de-rol, lol-de-rol, lol-de-rol, diddle-lol."

"I object to politics," said a fat, over-fed-looking gentleman. "I hold that a Tory is as good as any other man if not better."

"Don't blame me, sir," replied the guard. "Pitch into the cove as wrote the song, if you can find him. But to make a finish of it:

"When Peter the Great came over to welt us,
　With Henry the Eighth, and Boney to boot,
His most valiant soldiers, the moment they smelt
　　us,
　Were struck with such horror — pooh! they
　　couldn't shoot.
Then hurrah for Old England! She has boney fide
　A standard of liberty, which when unfurled
Will govern the ocean. And she's in a tidy
Good sort of way to welt the whole world.
　Tol-de-rol, lol-de-rol, lol-de-rol, diddle-lol."

"I should like to have a copy of that song," said a man with a pear-shaped nose and goggling eyes.

"I'm willing to oblige you; but why do you want it?" the guard replied.

"Because it is the greatest rubbish I ever listened to," the passenger returned. "If you haven't anything better than that to make a noise about, put your head in a sack and keep it there."

"Same to you and many of 'em," said the guard, nettled at the contemptuous reception of his ditty. "P'raps you're a musician yourself. You've got an instrument on your face that ought to play a good tune."

"I'll report you for insolence," said the passenger.

"Do, sir, do," replied the guard. "The more bothers we gets into the more wages we gets. The gov'nor hates milk-and-water sort of chaps, and he'd forgive us if we happened to drop a passenger or two into the road occasionally."

The gentleman with more than his share of nasal organ took the hint, and subsided into wrathful silence.

"What's the use of makin' a fuss when there's nothin' to make a fuss about?" said the coachman, anxious to make peace. "My mate means well, although he has a cur'us way of doin' it. You see that church?" pointing with his whip. "People say it's haunted by the ghost of a miser, who starved his wife and children to death, and drowned hisself in a well. I've never seen anything myself, but the 'osses prick their ears every time they pass the graveyard. You watch 'em!"

"Hang me, if such talk as this isn't worse than the idiotic song," the large-nosed gentleman remarked. "I've travelled thousands of miles, and the only thing I ever saw to scare me was a——"

"Whoa! Steady!" roared the coachman, putting a tight grip on the reins. "Darn your skins, what are you up to now?"

The horses were not only pricking their ears, but plunging violently. One of the wheelers nearly got a leg over the pole, and the leader danced and capered about in the most remarkable manner.

The coachman threw all his strength into his whip arm. His face was white, and his limbs were trembling when the horses dashed past the churchyard.

"I'll never tell that story ag'in as long as I live," he said. "Blow me, if I don't b'lieve that the 'osses understood what I said, and took fright! Hallo! What's that?"

"It sounded like somethin' droppin' out of a tree to the ground," the guard replied. "Love of my life, it's laughin' now!"

"Laughin'!" The coachman instinctively put a check on the horses, and then all sat still and listened. "Laughin'! I call it a howl. It's some animal as has got out of a cage. Spare us! How dark it's got all of a sudden!"

They had reached a part where three roads branched, and the coachman, allowing the horses to proceed at a walk, leaned forward and strained his eyes.

Overhead, the trees nearly met, and so profound was the silence that the passengers could hear the beating of their own hearts.

"Get along!" said the guard, nervously. "What's the use of starin' when there's nothin' to be seen?"

"I tell you—— Good Lord, here it comes!" the coachman gasped.

A form, dark and shadowy, coming from where no one could tell, just topped a wheel and flew over the coach, alighting with a curious spring sound on the other side.

The guard, uttering an oath, thrust his hand into a tool-box, fetched out a pistol, and fired it at random, while the large-nosed man snatched something near him and flung it wildly from the coach.

Down came a window, and a silvery voice exclaimed:

"What has happened? Are we attacked?"

"Don't be alarmed, ladies," replied the guard, holding his chin to keep his teeth from chattering. "The pistol went off—by—oh, lor'—accident!"

"Gentlemen!" said the coachman, "keep still. We've got somethin' to deal with that none of us understand. If," he added, looking over his shoulder, "any man here has done anything likely to raise the——"

The climax came. Again the shadowy form appeared, alighted for a moment on the coach, bounded over it, and vanished.

Then the coachman lashed his horses until the mad galloping made the coach roll and lurch dangerously. The passengers huddled together with no power to shout, and scarcely daring to speak.

Suddenly the reins tightened, and the horses came to a standstill. The coachman had succumbed, and leaned back, swooning.

The guard climbed over the seats, and pulled the coachman's ears until he came round.

"Jem," he said, faintly, "what was it? A bull on his hind legs, or a flyin' halligator? Oh, Jem! I fear it was the Old 'Un! I 'adn't time to notice his 'orns, 'oofs, and tail."

Again one of the windows came down, and a voice said:

"Have we reached Stowmarket?"

"No, miss," replied the guard. "To tell you the truth, we nearly reached a place where I hope none of us will ever go to."

"What is the matter?"

"That is what I cannot make out," said a voice.

The guard looked down, and saw a gentleman clad in black, with a short cloak wrapped closely about his shoulders.

"Where did you spring from?" the guard demanded.

"From the Mellis Road," the gentleman replied. "I came up just in time to stop the horses from running away. What, in the name of wonder, is all this about?"

"It means that we've had Spring-heeled Jack jumpin' on us like a devil on two sticks," the coachman said, through his chattering teeth.

"Impossible!" the stranger replied. "Fudge and fiddlesticks! You have been frightened by a shadow caused by the lamps or a passing cloud."

Here all the outside passengers lifted up their voices and declared that all had seen Spring-heeled Jack, and that, if the coach did not go straight on to Stowmarket without a moment's delay, each and every one would bring an action for damages.

No one thought of going back for what they had thrown from the coach, not even a dark, saturnine-looking man of military bearing.

"Well," said the gentleman, "this is the strangest story I ever heard. I am bound for Stowmarket—in fact, I was waiting for the coach; so, with your permission, I'll jump up. Ladies, don't be frightened. If Spring-heeled Jack comes this way again I have a remarkably fine brace of pistols, and he shall have the full benefit of them."

The saturnine-looking man raised his head.

"I have heard your voice somewhere," he said.

"It is common enough, like my name," the stranger replied, settling himself in a seat. "Drive on, coachman. There's a resident magistrate at Stowmarket, and you had better tell him the story. Spring-heeled Jack! I heard some idle people speaking about him to-night, but paid no heed to their talk."

The horses were already in motion, and as

the guard, shivering in his boots, climbed into his place, he said:

"There's two or three young ladies inside: Miss Helen Meadows, of Crowle Park, and her maid, who don't look more worried about this 'ere than if they was eatin' bread-and-jam. I can't make women out, and never could. They'll scream like whole cages of parrots at the sight of a mouse, but when Old Nick appears they sit still and put him to shame. Women is mysteries!"

Stowmarket at last, and no sooner was the "Crown" reached than the coachman and the guard and the passengers ran into the house, declaring that all the money that ever came out of the Mint, or that would come from it, would not tempt them to go another yard that night.

Spring-heeled Jack! Spring-heeled Jack! There was magic in the name now. Who was he? What was he? Where did he come from? What was his mission?

Such were the questions that went from mouth to mouth.

"If," said the coachman, pushing the large-nosed man aside as he reached the bar—"if I didn't feel all of a jelly-like, I'd only have my usual 'lowance of rum; but as it is, I must have a double quantity. My mate, who plays so beautiful on the brass pea-shooter, will pay."

The guard looked askance, but it was not the time to quibble over a shilling, so he paid with a good grace, and, pulling the coachman's sleeve, whispered:

"Just see how the milingtary-lookin' man is eyein' the gent we picked up on the road. Something happened with Miss Meadows just now, only she looked at him in a different kind o' way, and I'll swear I heard her sigh."

"Single women sigh when they are in love, and married ones sigh when they can't have what other women weary of," the coachman remarked.

Just then there was a terrific uproar in the room where the passengers had taken shelter. The soldierly-like man had gone outside to make certain inquiries, and running back in a fury, seized upon the large-nosed man.

"I forgot it for the moment," he gasped. "It was under my feet, and you were sitting next to me. Where is it, you scoundrel? If you threw it off the coach, I'll——"

"Threw what?" roared the violently-shaken man. "Help! help!"

"I'll help you, as sure as my name is Tench!" retorted the other. "Only you could have done it. Where is my valise? It contained notes and gold to the value of four hundred guineas, belonging to my master, Colonel Manfred."

"Gently! gently!" said the landlord, running between them. "Don't kill the man. Are you sure that you have overhauled the coach?"

"Quite sure!" said Tench stammering the words through his white lips. "When Spring-heeled Jack, or whatever it was, came kicking up his infernal heels round us, this idiot threw my valise into the road."

"In that case, it must be lying somewhere in the road," said the stranger who had joined the coach where the road branched. "Mr. Tench, I am willing to go with you to help to find it."

A shadow, like a mask, came over Tench's face.

"Thank you," he said. "May I ask your name?"

"Wrong—Harry Wrong. I am fairly well known in the county of Essex."

"Wrong! Humph! that is a peculiar name." He looked uneasy, and then, falling back, looked steadily at the man.

"Yes, it is a peculiar name, but as I did not choose it, I must put up with it. Bring a lantern here. You people seem to be all sixes and sevens, and don't know what you are doing. Come on, Mr. Tench."

The guard supplied the lamp, and Wrong took it, saying:

"I should like to meet this mysterious being, Spring-heeled Jack. Do you think his idea was robbery?"

Tench was too intent upon his loss to reply coherently, and muttered something beneath his breath.

Side by side they walked up the road, scarcely exchanging a word for more than two miles.

"Here is the spot where I stopped the horses," Wrong said.

He turned, spread out his cloak, and turned again. Tench uttered a cry of horror at the change that had come over his companion.

His eyes were no longer soft and kind, but gleaming with a fierce light. His face had become fiendish with painted eyebrows, and stiff, bristling moustache. His hands had grown larger, and the nails of his fingers were long and hooked.

"Spring-heeled Jack, by all that is horrible!" Tench cried, dropping on his knees.

"Yes, I am Spring-heeled Jack!" cried the being. "I am Spring-heeled Jack, and you are Marcus Tench, slave and dupe of Colonel Manfred, his liar-in-chief, as you always were, and one of the greatest villains unhanged. I am the avenger of wrong—the avenger of the man who suffered so much from such perjured lips as yours. Dog! prepare to die!"

"No, no!" Tench pleaded. "I implore you not to kill me! Give me time to repent!"

"Repent! The meaning of such a word is unknown to you. But I will not kill you now. You shall bear Spring-heeled Jack's brand until he comes to you for the last time!"

Spring-heeled Jack pounced on the shuddering man, and presently a cry of agony rang through the air. Something seemed to sear into Marcus Tench's brain, and, flinging up his arms, he fell, and lay like a dead man.

Consciousness returned. He opened his eyes, scrambled to his feet, and looked hazily about him.

Soon came the memory of what had happened. His teeth chattered and his blood froze, but soon a great joy came into his heart.

Within a few yards of him lay the missing

valise, and, seizing it, he ran madly back to Stowmarket.

Covered with dust, and perspiring from every pore in his skin, he burst into the hostelry.

"Merciful Heaven!" cried the innkeeper, "what is that as red as blood on your forehead? It is the letter 'S,' and clean-cut as if a surgeon had done it!"

CHAPTER V.

The Crypt.—A Good Master and a Faithful Servant.—The Watchers of the Night.

In an arched crypt, deep down beneath a mansion, sat a young man with his hands resting on his knees. At his feet lay a pickaxe, and a lantern shining upon a quantity of newly turned earth, showing how he had been working.

Near the mound stood a small iron-bound box, secured with a strong bar of steel and two padlocks.

The woodwork was worm-eaten, and the metal so rusty that it would require but a blow to burst it asunder and reveal the contents of the box.

"It is time that he was here," the man said.

He put his hand to his ear and listened, and then creeping softly to the base of a spiral staircase, seemingly hewn out of the solid wall, he held his breath, and put his hand to his ear.

"No," he murmured, "it was only the wind. I wish he would come. Never have I been so anxious to run such risks. Hark! That sounds like his signal—and it is!"

Light footsteps sounded on the stairs, and presently Bertram Wraydon entered the crypt.

"Another find, Denis?" he said. "You are a wonder——"

"And a wonder has been wondering what on earth had become of you," Denis replied. "Yes, another find. Gems, I expect, this time, or maybe family papers, or some such rubbish, because the box is so light."

"Family papers are not rubbish, Denis Stocks," Bertram Wraydon said, laughing.

"That may be so, from your point of view," Denis returned. "Well, I suppose not; but as such things are not in my line, I don't know. My father didn't worry himself about my education. With all his faults he wasn't a bad sort."

"I suppose not," Bertram Wraydon remarked, sinking on one knee and examining the box. "Judging by what his son is, he must have been a very good fellow."

"Ah, sir, you're a-trying to flatter me ag'in, but it won't do. If I was as bad as," smiling, "what they say Spring-heeled Jack is, how could I but help being true and faithful to you? Don't I remember the time when I, a poor soldier lad, lay wounded, that you went a mile under fire to fetch me some water, and carried me in your arms while the bullets rattled about you like a hailstorm? Can I forget?"

"There! There!" said Bertram Wraydon. "You were talking about your father."

"Oh, him!" Denis said, laughing and wiping his eyes at the same time. "Well, he had his funny ways. He'd come home on Saturday night and knock us all down like skittles, and then treat us to a supper of pork chops and onions. There was a father for you, if you like!"

"The pork chops and onions sound well, but I might have objected to the knocking-down business," Bertram remarked.

"No doubt," said Denis, untying a parcel Wraydon had brought into the crypt; "but that was my father's way of making himself agreeable, and he couldn't alter it now if he would, because he's dead and gone. You don't seem to be in a hurry to open the box."

"It can wait until we have had our supper. I am sure you want yours badly enough," Bertram replied.

He took from his pocket a piece of old parchment filled with small writing and queer-looking marks, and glancing at it, nodded his head.

"Both papers and gems," he said. "Denis, you and I will be rich one day, richer even than Hubert Sedgefield."

"Don't mention that name to me, or you will drive me mad," Denis Stocks said, clutching the handle of the pickaxe. "The measly thief! The liar! The coward!"

"Give him rope enough, and he will hang himself."

"And these are the hands that would like to send him swinging," Denis said. "Sit down, sir. There's the three-legged stool; the ground is good enough for me."

"Help yourself," said Wraydon, pointing to a cold fowl and a crusty loaf. "There's wine to-night, and we'll drink to each other in bumpers. Last night, I had a stroke of luck."

"Ah! luck! I know the sort of luck you had. Well, well! I suppose it will come all right in the end."

"If you can get Old Father Time to turn over a few advance leaves of his book, I will tell you," Bertram Wraydon remarked.

Denis Stocks whistled softly to himself as he went to a niche, and returned with some knives and forks, two scrupulously clean plates, a pepper-pot, and a salt-cellar.

"Your share," continued Wraydon, "is just two hundred and fifty pounds."

"Two hundred and fifty fardens, you mean," said Denis, grinning. "What good is money to me, do you think? If I had pockets full of it, I should only go about jingling like a lot of sledge-bells. The only thing I hope for, think about in the daytime, and dream about at night, is seeing you restored to the ownership of Wraydon House, and me your very humble and faithful servant."

Bertram Wraydon grasped the man's hand.

"You are the best and dearest fellow in all

the world," Wraydon said. "What I should do without you, is more than I can tell."

"Well," said Denis, pausing with a piece of fowl on his fork, "perhaps what my father taught me has come in handy. The secret has passed from father to son for hundreds of years, but I never thought it would ever be of much use. You see," pointing to the other side of the crypt, "I have rigged up a forge, and shall start making another."

"The one I am wearing now has caused some astonishment," Wraydon said, smiling.

He took a bullet from his pocket and handed it to Denis, who looked critically at it.

"Out of a gun with a pretty stiff groove," he said. "Did it hit you square?"

"Fair and square," Wraydon replied. "And only two hours ago. The gentleman who fired it is now lying on his back with his legs in the air, and it will be some time before he knows where he is."

"You didn't——" said Denis Stocks. "What I mean to say is——"

"I know exactly what you mean to say," Wraydon interrupted. "Put your mind at rest. He was only an interfering fool, without a penny in his pocket. Denis, there's no need for that; we have more money, as yet, than we know what to do with."

"What about the two hundred and fifty pounds you want to give me? Twice that amount makes five hundred, and it's a tidy sum to pick up in a single night, my master."

"Oh, that's quite a different matter, as I will tell you by-and-by," said Bertram Wraydon. "Someone you know will go short of it, and another man you remember well, got much more than he expected."

Denis Stocks rubbed the tip of his nose, and his eyes twinkled comically.

"Well, I suppose it is no use talking of these things," he remarked. "I leave it all to you. Now, master, I want to know where I am to get to work? To tell you the truth, I find it a bit lonely down here. I don't grumble; I'd work in a coal-mine all my life to serve you, but I've been used to the sunlight, and I don't mind telling you that this old crypt is a little ghostly. I think of them Cavaliers coming down in the dead of night to hide their treasures so that the Puritans should not grab them with their greedy fingers. I think of the poor gentlemen, stiff, stark, and dead on the battle-field, and somehow, when I think that their spirits must come back to the place where they were so jolly and happy, I feel creepy."

"I shall have plenty of work for you to do presently," Wraydon said, filling two horn cups with wine. "Here's success to ourselves and confusion to our enemies."

They drank, Denis deeply, with a relish, and smacking his lips.

"Now go to bed, and I'll keep watch," Wraydon said. "Not that I think we shall be disturbed; but it is just as well to be on the safe side."

"But you are tired. I—— Master, how is it that I cannot meet your eyes when you fix them earnestly on me? I—— Heigho!"

He yawned, and his head began to roll on his shoulders.

"Go to bed," said Wraydon, gently, but firmly.

"Yes, yes, I'm going," Denis said, rubbing his eyes as he rose wearily to his feet. "I—I do believe that you can—heigho!—send me to sleep when you like."

Bertram Wraydon took Denis by the arm, and led him to a corner where there were two mattresses side by side, and plenty of blankets.

"I'll not take the trouble to undress to-night," Denis said, reeling on his feet. "The wine must have got into my head. There's plenty of oil in the lamp, so——"

He flopped heavily down on the mattress, thrust his right arm under his head, and in a moment he was sound asleep.

Bertram Wraydon then went to the box, and prized it open with an iron bar.

The hollow lid was packed closely with linen, pressing down sundry pieces of wool. Wraydon took them out one by one, and disclosed a score or more rare gems, some loose, some set in rings. There was also a magnificent diamond necklace, with an emerald pendant.

"Mine!" he said. "Mine! So I feel no pang of conscience in taking them, but I'll not sell a single one, so long as I have a guinea in my pocket. Heyday! I wonder what my great-grandfather and great-grandmother would think if they knew to what a pass a Wraydon had come? And I, an outcast, living under the shadow of the gallows. The baseness of it! The villainy of it! When I think—— Hush! I will work out my revenge!"

Beneath the gems lay a quantity of old letters and a parchment deed. Bertram placed them under the unoccupied mattress, and the gems in his pocket.

Then, glancing from the staircase to Denis's sleeping form, he said:

"I shall be safe for an hour, but I will be no longer. I would not have Denis miss me for worlds!"

Leaving Bertram Wraydon for a time, we return to Wraydon House.

Hubert Sedgefield was at his town house in London, and his servants had gone with him, leaving three men as caretakers.

They, respectively named Poley, Jaggers, and Rickers, had been specially selected for the work. Sedgefield had been plain with them so far in saying that someone had stolen into the gallery and given him a fright, whereat Poley, Jaggers, and Rickers, being armed with pistols and cudgels, and instructed to use them in the event of another visitation, swore that they would batter, riddle, and pulverise the bones and body of any intruder until his mother should not know him from an Egyptian mummy.

Like men of their class, they made free use of the house and everything they could find in it. They dived into the wine-cellars, gave extensive orders to the tradesmen instructed to call, and slept in the softest beds.

No servants'-hall for them! Was it likely, when there were so many fine rooms at their command?

One night, when they had gone round the house, testing the security of every door and window, Poley suggested that they should adjourn to the drawing-room.

"That's going a bit too far, ain't it?" said Jaggers. "Them gilt-backed, spindle-legged chairs weren't made for the likes of me."

"There's the couches, carpets, rugs, and sich-like," Poley replied. "What do you say, Rickers?"

Rickers shook his head, and then, placing his hands under his chin, balanced it. It was a large head, nearly round, exceedingly fat; in fact, it was a colossal head, and once set rolling, there was no telling where it might not go to, if not checked in time.

"I'm agreeable to anything," Rickers replied. "I'm the sort of man as can make myself agreeable anywhere and with anybody; but supposin' we should upset any gin or beer over the carpets and couldn't get the stains out, the squire would swear until he couldn't see out of his eyes!"

"Let him swear!" said Poley, snapping his fingers. "We've got a long job here, and a fine one, too, if we all stick together. All we've got to do is to hatch up some nice ghost-stories and to blow out one or two o' the windows with our pistols, and the squire'll keep away. Besides, he's goin' to Dover."

"I was brought up to tell the truth and shame Beelzebub," Rickers said, solemnly. "My mother taught me them words while I was weighin' up the sugar in pounds, with two thick pieces of brown paper to each."

"Pickles!" said Poley, contemptuously.

"Oh, yes," replied Rickers, brightening up. "We sold pickles—cabbage and honions in pen'orths, and if they went a bit musty, we shoved in lots of pepper to sharpen 'em up a bit. Oh, dear! what a wicked world it is! Well, I'll give way. Anything for peace, is my motter."

"What was your mother when you was in gaol?" demanded Poley, savagely. "Come, none of your hypocrisy. We'll go down, fetch up the beer and gin, and then make ourselves jolly!"

At this, all three laughed. Poley was the leading spirit, and in the end had his way in everything.

Having provided themselves with liquor sufficient to set the heads of a dozen men humming, they repaired to the handsomely-furnished drawing-room.

Rickers lit the candles, Jaggers drew the curtains cosily, and Poley looked after the refreshment department.

"Now I feel like Joolius Seizer," he said, sinking into a chair and thrusting his heels into the carpeted floor. "Rickers, how would you like to be a swell? Look at this 'ere table, inlaid with pearl," rapping it with his grimy knuckles. "It must have cost a fortune."

"Two hundred guineas, you dirty vagabond!"

"Two hundred guineas," repeated Poley. "Who are you calling a vagabond?"

"I ain't calling anybody a vagabond," Rickers remarked, sampling the beer by swallowing a glassful and quickly filling another.

"Then it was you, Jaggers," said Poley.

Jaggers liked his gin neat, although it made his nose blue and his eyes stare blearily. He had his mouth full just then, so, instead of replying, he shook his head.

"Go it!" said Poley. "Perhaps you'll tell me next that I can't believe my own ears. I s'pose them gilt figgers on the clock spoke!"

"Very likely," said a voice.

Poley seemed to turn to mottled soap, and sat gasping at a gilt "Ajax defying the Lightning" from the top of the magnificent clock.

"I say," he said, in a hoarse whisper, "did you hear that?"

"I heard you say 'very likely,' replied Rickers, still intent on reducing the stock of beer.

"Of course you did!" Jaggers chimed in. "I heard you, too, and then you looked at the clock as if you'd like to steal it."

"I? Why, I!" cried Poley—"I never said such a thing! What's that?"

Someone was tapping softly at the door.

"Go-o-o and see who it is, Jaggers," stammered Rickers, as his hair began to rise.

"Who are you, to order me about?" demanded Rickers, with a chalky face. "Go and see yourself!"

Tap, tap, tap!

Poley sat still, grasping the arms of his chair.

"It must be the wind," he said, hoarsely.

"It is not the wind," replied a voice.

The door opened, and a face, hideous and contorted, looked in, then vanished in an instant.

Rickers indulged in a wholesale groan, and shot under the table and hid his face.

The feelings of the other two were indescribable. Completely spellbound, they seemed fixed to their chairs.

Poley was the first to speak.

"Jaggers," he said, "you have your pistols. Fire a shot hrough the door."

But Jaggers only made faces, drew his legs up, waggled his feet, and seemed to be drifting into a state of idiocy.

The door opened again, and a long black arm came in, and after flourishing wildly, disappeared.

"Jaggers!" Poley shrieked, "rouse yourself! It must be a lark! Them village boys are up to all sorts of games. Some warmint's got into the house and—— Oh, lor! murder!"

The door swung back and struck the wall with a crash. In it was framed the fearsome figure of Spring-heeled Jack!

"Avaunt! Quit this place, or die!" he cried.

Poley snatched a pistol and fired, but so wild was his aim that he struck a candelabrum and smashed it out of all shape.

The room was now in semi-darkness, and Poley, feeling that he was going mad himself, clutched at the glasses and bottles on the tables and hurled them at—nothing!

Spring-heeled Jack was no longer in the doorway, and Poley, the bravest of the three, rushed out on the landing. To his amazement and alarm, so much that his heart rose in his mouth, he saw the appalling figure leap up the staircase at a single bound, and then, hanging its head over the balustrade, grin hideously at him.

"Come on," yelled Poley, dashing down the staircase—"this is no place for us! Come on, unless you want to turn to brimstone and fire! The house is haunted by the Evil One!"

Jaggers was on his heels in a moment, but Rickers was not so lucky. It took time to crawl from under the table.

"Don't leave me here!" he whined, with his eyes still shut. "I am coming as fast as I can! Poley! Jaggers! I shall have a heap of money when my Aunt Sairey dies, and she's eighty-ni——"

Not daring to raise his face, he reached the landing on his hands and knees, tipped over, shot down in double-quick time, and overtook Jaggers.

He not only overtook him, but caught him in the middle of the back, with the result that, to save himself, he threw his arms round Poley's neck, and Rickers took a violent fancy to Jaggers's legs.

What all three said just then cannot be recorded, but it was free and emphatic.

Never since the day that tumbling downstairs was invented did a bundle of men, locked in a frantic and confused embrace, ever travel so quickly.

A mass of waving legs and arms, bumped heads, and twisted bodies, they reached the hall.

"Take your head out of my chest!" Poley gasped, aiming a weak and ineffectual blow at Jaggers.

"I will when you take the heel of your boot out of my eye!" Jaggers snarled.

"You've got your elbow in my mouth," Rickers mumbled. "Marcy! here he comes again!"

It was not Spring-heeled Jack, but only his voice.

It roared, in bursts of blood-curdling laughter, down the staircase.

"Hirelings! Villains! Cowards!" it yelled, "this place is mine! I, Spring-heeled Jack, am master here! Ha, ha, ha!"

How Poley, Jaggers, and Rickers got up, made for the front-door, and plunged headlong into the open air they never knew, but presently they stood in the bright moonlight, clinging to each other for support and panting for breath.

Then with one accord they went racing across the park. Rickers had always been good at the running away business, especially when there was a fair stand-up fight going on, and he was first in the village, waving his arms and shouting, "Spring-heeled Jack! Spring-heeled Jack!"

The constable happened to be coming round a corner, and meeting Rickers full butt, another catastrophe took place.

Poley and Jaggers arrived, and picked up a somewhat mangled constable, with a nose that had spread with alarming and painful suddenness all over his face; one eye blackened up, and the other going round and round as though upon a swivel.

It was found that the constable had only one boot on. How the other had come off, or where it had gone to, no one could tell, and Rickers did not stop to make inquiries.

Raising himself up from the earth, he cried:

"Serve you right; what do you mean by bu'stin' round corners at the rate of ten miles an hour?" and made the best of his way out of the place.

The constable was dazed as well as sorely smitten. He saw all sorts of curious things, and imagined that he was flying through the air with a seven-pound weight hanging to his nose.

By degrees his vision cleared, and he beheld Poley and Jaggers growing out of a sort of red mist.

"What was it?" he said, "a brick or a turnip?"

Here was an opportunity not to be lost, and Poley at once improved upon it.

"I saw him do it," he said. "If he hadn't taken to his heels, I'd have given him a oner for himself."

"Who?" demanded the constable, taking out his handkerchief and nursing his nose tenderly.

"A cove in a slouched hat and smock-frock," Poley replied.

The description being vague, the constable reflected.

"Red hair and a green patch over one eye?" he asked.

"That's him," said Poley; "you've got him to a T."

"Bill Spudge promised me something for myself whenever he met me in the dark," the constable said, "and Bill Spudge will find himself in clink before he's an hour older."

There was a somewhat jovial company at the "Rosebush" Inn. It was Peter Bloggs's birthday, and naturally enough the regular customers looked to him to stand treat.

So Peter in the openness of his heart brewed several jorums of old ale, ginger, and sugar, and soon the festivities got into full swing.

"Let's have the 'Blood Drinker's Dream,'" said Bloggs. "I like that part where the ghosts of his wictims come in all of a row and send him into fits."

A man with feet out of all proportion to his thin legs stood up, and, striking an attitude, began:

"The red wintry moon was driftin' o'er the mountings——"

He got no further. Sam Bullifant rushed in, hit him over the head with a stick, clutched him by the throat, and bundled him into a corner.

"Spudge, you willain," said the constable, "I've got you!"

Dazed, and completely bewildered at the suddenness of the attack, and with the "Blood Drinker's Dream" still in his mind, Spudge murmured:

"The red wintry moon was driftin'——"

"I'll drift you into the lock-up, so come along!" roared the constable.

"What's the matter?" demanded Peter Bloggs. "What are you knockin' the man about for? He's done nothin' but sit here since six."

"Since when?—since six?" Bullifant gasped.

"Yes, ask the others. Put us all on our alfred davids. Bully, you're drunk; you've been drunk ever since Spring-heeled Jack was seen."

"The red misty moon was driftin' o'er the mountings," Spudge repeated, in a helpless sort of manner, with his eyes closed.

"Spudge is going silly," a man cried. "Give him somethin' to drink. If that won't bring him round, he'll die."

"And Bully will be his murderer; we'll all go to see him hanged," Peter Bloggs remarked. "It will be a grand day for the willage people."

"No, no," groaned the constable, sinking into a chair. "Spudge's got a thick head, and he'll come round if you leave him alone. There's been a mistake, a terrible mistake."

"Sich a one as 'll cost you a crown at the least," Bloggs remarked, with an eye to business.

"I—I met," said the constable, mopping his face with a handkerchief not quite so red as his face, "two of them chaps who are lookin' after the squire's house, and——"

The door opened, and a voice came through it.

"They will never go there again," it said.

Bloggs ran to the door.

"There's no one here," he said, screwing his head round with a mighty effort; "not even a shadder."

"The air is full o' mysteries," the constable said. "Peter, I'll stay, if you don't mind. Spudge, give me your hand. I always liked you, you know I did."

Spudge, now in his right senses, had his doubts about the constable's affection, but as more "hot pot" was being brewed, he forgot and forgave, and later on thundered out the "Blood Drinker's Dream" with great effect.

Poley nudged Jaggers, and suggesting that Bill Spudge ought to be hanged without going before a jury, they left the constable nursing his nose and his revenge.

CHAPTER VI.
Colonel Manfred is Troubled in his Mind, and Interviews a Celebrated Man.

NIGHT had fallen over London. The watchmen, called "Charlies," were buttoning up their great-coats, as was their custom, no matter whether the weather was stifling hot or freezing cold.

In those days the safety of London was left principally to these decrepit old men, who went wheezing and coughing, swinging a lantern in one hand, and thumping a staff with the other.

The Charlie also carried a wooden rattle, which when whirled in the air awoke the just, and gave ample warning to the thief.

Charlie had also a sentry-box placed at a certain part of his beat, and it was his custom, when everyone who ought to be in bed had gone there, to shut himself up in the box and snore until the morning.

The wind had whipped the streets clean of litter, and went whistling up and down courts and alleys like so many exasperating boys with a new tune in their heads.

There was a freshness in the air, and that peculiar smell that tells of coming rain. It stole through a window in an old house at the back of Gray's Inn Road, and brought in with it a whiff of the not then far off country, of freshly-carted hay, and roses and honeysuckle that clustered over cottage doors.

"I wonder," said Colonel Manfred, crossing the room to close the window, for the wind had set the candle sputtering and guttering, "I wonder what has become of Tench? I expected him two days ago, and he is conspicuous by his absence.

"Sanders!" he cried, ringing a hand-bell.

A strange, lopsided-looking man entered the room, crab-like, with his arms hanging straight at his sides.

"Go to the coach office, and see if you can learn anything about Tench," the colonel said.

"He is already here," Sanders replied, with a peculiar look in his peculiar eyes.

"Then why the deuce does he not come to me?"

"Colonel," said Sanders, "there is something the matter with Marcus Tench. He has met with an extraordinary adventure, and—and a mark is set upon his brow."

"The mark of Cain, I should not wonder," muttered the colonel. "If the rascal had his deserts he would have got his head through a halter long ago." Then, aloud: "Send him to me at once! But stay, Sanders! Tench should have a valise with him."

"He has it with him, but he tells me that he has lost the key."

"There are other things besides a key to open a valise with," snapped the colonel. "Send him to me at once!"

A few moments later Marcus Tench shuffled into the room with the valise in one hand, and the other on his brow.

"What ails you?" demanded the colonel. "Have you had a fall?"

"Such a one as I shall never get over," Tench replied, with a moan, as he sank into a chair. "I fell into the hands of Spring-heeled Jack. Look here!" removing his hand from his forehead.

"Merciful powers! this is awful!" the

This reply, given in a cool, off-handed manner, and without removing the flower from his mouth, rather staggered Colonel Manfred, and he, for the moment, was at a loss what to say.

Townsend came to his rescue.

"Come into my room, and alone," he said. "Your man can stay outside. I never deal with a third party, unless I find it absolutely necessary. Two witnesses are never put in the box at the same time, eh, colonel?"

"No. Quite right," the colonel replied. "You know me by sight, of course?"

"I know," returned Townsend, as he ushered his visitor into a plainly-furnished room, "a great deal about you, Colonel Manfred, and I think I can tell what has brought you here. Spring-heeled Jack, eh?"

"You must be a wizard!" cried Colonel Manfred.

"Not quite. News travels quickly, even from Stowmarket," Townsend said. "Heard all about what happened to your man. Well, let me have the story from your lips."

The colonel rattled it off, while Townsend sat apparently listening indifferently.

"So you've lost your money, and your man's got a letter S to remind him of Spring-heeled Jack," Townsend remarked, when the colonel had finished speaking. "Is that all?"

"Gadzooks! is it not enough?" demanded the colonel.

"It might have been worse because it might have spelt murder," Townsend replied, quite calmly. "Excuse me, there's a bluebottle on the wall, and he must find some other place to sing his buzzing song, or die."

Colonel Manfred began to fume and grow very red in the face.

"Mr. Townsend," he said, "I did not expect to be treated in this manner!"

"Eh? What's that?" Townsend exclaimed. "Oh, I see! You expect me to deliver my judgment. No, no! I never do that. I act, not talk. You go home, and I will come to your house—I know perfectly well where you live—about midnight. Something may happen before then."

"What is likely to happen?" asked the colonel, feeling that his brain was getting addled.

"How should I know? Heaps of things. Excuse me, but I'm busy. I always am. I don't envy a lazy man, but I should dearly like a holiday sometimes. Sunday and weekdays are all the same to me. The only relaxation I have had for years was when a fool of a country constable locked me up in mistake for a horse-stealer. There! There! Didn't I tell you that I was busy?"

So saying he opened the door, and Colonel Manfred passed out as if he were treading on a red-hot floor.

"Tench," he said, "is that coach still waiting?"

"And likely to wait," Tench replied. "No sooner did we get out than both horses fell down."

"Then call another," said the colonel. "I don't know what to make of all this."

They drove back to the quiet street leading out of Gray's Inn Road, and no sooner were they in the house than Sanders said:

"There's been a gentleman to see you, sir."

"What sort of a gentleman?"

"Tall, dark, and good-looking. He did not leave any name, but said he might be able to call again. If not he said that you would probably remember your old friend Plyers, who helped you and Mr. Sedgefield to rob Mr. Wraydon. Don't blame me!" The colonel had raised his hand as if to strike him. "That was the message, word for word, he told me to deliver."

"And you let him go with such words on his lips?" roared the colonel.

"What was I to do?" Sanders rejoined. "I couldn't hold him. He was not the sort of man I'd care to tackle. He was a young giant in stature, and such eyes! They seemed to look through and through me."

"Perhaps Wraydon himself," Colonel Manfred muttered. "Townsend may be able to kill two birds with one stone. Curses on all these mysteries, I like them not! Come upstairs with me, Tench. I have something to say to you before the officer arrives."

"So have I to you," Tench said. "To tell you the truth—— But I will wait until we can talk with closed doors."

Sanders, the lopsided, grinned, and thrust his tongue into his cheek.

"There they go, the pair of beauties!" he said. "They think that I know nothing, but they are mistaken, and if I don't get my whack out of this little business, I'll know the reason why."

On entering the room Colonel Manfred wheeled round and faced Marcus Tench.

"You wish to leave me," he said. "I see it in your eyes."

"You have read my thoughts correctly," Tench replied. "I am not a coward, but these new horrors are more than I can contend with. You speak of Bertram Wraydon as being alive, but I do not believe it. He is dead, and has sent a devil in the form of Spring-heeled Jack to torture us."

"You talk foolishly," the colonel replied. "Wraydon is alive, and has been well-informed. Hitchman, from Colchester, knew him well, and swears that he saw him at Ipswich, although only for a moment."

"Hitchman would swear to anything for money," Tench said. "He has fastened himself like a barnacle on Squire Sedgefield, and will take a lot of shaking before he is got rid of."

"You will not convince me," the colonel returned. "Wraydon is alive, and in England. Philbrick knows where to find him. So while we are looking for Wraydon we must keep a watchful eye on the barrister. Philbrick could tell us something about Wraydon's escape if he liked, but these accursed lawyers are like oysters. Even when you force their mouths open they are dumb. Tench, put aside your fears, and remain with me. We are useful to each other."

The colonel pulled out a handsome, double gold-cased watch, and without troubling to open it touched a spring. The response came in a faint but musical chiming.

"A quarter to eleven," said the colonel. "I will go to my room and rest for an hour. And you?"

"I will remain where I am. The more light and warmth I have the better for me."

The colonel laughed in a mirthless way, and went to his room, a spacious and excellently-furnished chamber. The bed was hung with amber silk curtains, while the bed itself was as white as snow, soft and inviting.

Colonel Manfred merely removed his boots and coat, and lay down.

Something creaked. It might be a chair, a cabinet, for furniture has a trick of making uncanny sounds at night. Then came a rustling sound. Colonel Manfred opened his eyes and gasped for breath. The curtains were thrown back, and Spring-heeled Jack stood before him.

Just then Marcus Tench shouted up the staircase, "Mr. Townsend has come!" Colonel Manfred heard, but the words died out of his ears as, with a cry that had little human in it, he flung himself between the bed and the wall, and there lay writhing in the agonies of a fit.

Townsend, Tench, and Sanders heard the cry, and burst into the room.

"Raise him! Put him on the bed. Now lift his head," Townsend said. Great heavens, how bad he looks! Quick with some water. Dash it in his face. That's right. Now for some brandy. He will live."

"Little enough will he have to live for!" cried a sharp voice near the window.

Townsend swung round on his heels, and saw a face peering at him through the glass.

He slipped a pistol down his sleeve into his hand, but before he could use it, the room became filled with flame and smoke. A deafening report rang out, and then followed darkness and silence.

Townsend was the first to speak.

Used to face danger, even when it led him up to the gaping jaws of death, the appalling explosion and the ghastly face at the window thrilled him with horror.

"Limberham," he cried, hoarsely, "where are you? Are you hurt?"

For some moments there was no reply. The shock had stunned Limberham. But at length his answer came.

"I am near you, and not hurt," he said. "Merciful Heaven! the darkness is horrible! Bring a light."

Marcus Tench entered, bearing a candle in each hand. His face was ashy, and he trembled in every limb.

"The colonel!" he gasped—"is he dead? No; but look at him. Misery of miseries! look at him!"

The colonel lay on his back; his eyes rolled fearfully in his head, and his lips framed words that died away incoherently in his throat.

"Look to him," Townsend said, diving his hands into his pockets, and fetching out a brace of pistols. "Limberham, the face we saw at the window was Spring-heeled Jack's! Pull yourself together, man, and follow me!"

Placing his knee on the sill, he crawled out, and found himself on a lead-covered ledge forming a gutter. A narrow stone parapet prevented the storm-water from rushing into the street.

Townsend, supporting himself with one hand on the parapet, looked up. There was neither pipe nor anything that a man could cling to.

Forty feet down lay the street, lit here and there with flickering lamps that only deepened the black shadows cast by the old houses.

"Limberham," he said, "take care of yourself. Do not trust your weight on the parapet. It is as rotten as a pear in places. Steady, man! Place your hand on my shoulder."

"You shall go no further, I tell you," Limberham said, putting a fierce grip on his shoulder. "What is the use of throwing your life away?"

Townsend shook him off roughly, and, dropping on his knees, thrust out his arms.

"I can touch the other side," he said. "I'll stay here while you fetch a light."

Enraged at what he considered the foolish daring of his companion, Limberham swore under his breath, but he had no choice but to obey.

Returning to the window, he saw that Sanders had joined Tench, and both were bending over Colonel Manfred, who was breathing with difficulty and throwing his arms right and left.

"Fetch a lantern, one of you!" Limberham said. "Look sharp!"

Sanders fetched a lantern, and Limberham crept back to Townsend, who had changed his attitude to resting on one knee.

He crouched with a pistol in each hand, and as the light flashed on him, Limberham saw how white and yet how determined his face was.

"You have seen something?" Limberham said.

"No; but I have heard something," Townsend replied. "A voice has mocked me, bidding me go search for thieves and leave honest men alone. Give me the lantern. See! we can step over this space."

Scarcely had he ceased speaking when crack! went a pistol-like report, and the lantern smashed in his hand.

Something like a shadow was flitting between the wall and the parapet of the adjoining house, and Limberham, drawing his pistols, blazed away.

"Many thanks! Ha, ha, ha! No bullet cast by mortal can harm Spring-heeled Jack!"

The mocking voice and laughter were maddening to the two men.

"Go back!" cried the voice—"go back! Advance, and I will hurl you into the street."

"We are beaten," Townsend acknowledged. "We must return. Here we can do nothing."

"Nothing! Nothing!" repeated the voice out of the darkness.

By this time doors and windows were flying open, and affrighted people shouting for help.

Four doddering old "Charlies" came tottering up, but a word from Townsend brought them to a standstill.

"Stay where you are!" he cried. "Draw across the road, and let no man pass you."

In less than two minutes Townsend and Limberham joined the watchmen in the street.

"We have been hunting a burglar, and missed him," the chief officer said, in a tone of bitterness. "There is nothing more to be done, so you can go."

Just then a man attired in black strolled up.

"I met a man just now, running like the wind," he said.

"Which way did he go?" Townsend demanded.

"Towards the Foundling Hospital," the man replied. "Heels of Mercury! how the fellow ran! His feet scarcely touched the ground. He flew, I tell you. Are you looking for him?"

"To tell you the truth," Townsend replied, forcing a laugh, "I hardly know what I am looking for. Limberham, he has slipped through our fingers, so we had better take a parting look at Colonel Manfred, and see that one of his men fetches a doctor."

"S'life! he will need a clever one to bring him round to health and strength," Limberham muttered.

A dispute arose between Sanders and Tench as to who should fetch the doctor. Neither relished the idea of going out, but at length Townsend suggested that they should both go.

When they had gone, the two officers sat down and watched the colonel. He was calmer now, and lay exhausted and apparently asleep.

"You know something of this man?" Limberham whispered.

"I know nothing good of him," Townsend replied. "But that might be said of a good many men in London."

"There is a mystery here that requires some fathoming," Limberham remarked.

"It may not be so deep as you think," said Townsend, nursing his chin in the hollow of his hand. "Nevertheless, I am troubled in my mind. This creature who calls himself Spring-heeled Jack might as easily have blown our brains out as he did the lantern. The wonder of it is that he seemed to have no desire to do us an injury of any kind. Humph! you remember the celebrated Wraydon case?"

"Yes; but what on earth has that to do with Spring-heeled Jack?"

"Upon my word, I don't know," Townsend replied; "yet, from the moment I entered this house, it has been working in my mind. Colonel Manfred was a witness against Lieutenant Wraydon."

"A most reluctant one. He shed tears at the court-martial, I heard."

"You may have also heard that there are such things as crocodile tears," Townsend said.

"Pshaw! I must be wool-gathering. Listen! here come the two brave men with old Doctor Rankin. Hark how he thumps his walking-stick on the stairs! The old gentleman makes as much noise in a house as a clap of thunder when he is in a hurry. Limberham, while the doctor is attending to his patient, we may as well take a turn down Lamb's Conduit Street."

"The walk will do us good," Limberham replied. "You are a man of iron, but, to tell you the truth, I want a stroll to steady my nerves. I hate mysteries."

"Yonder we have one, then!" cried Townsend.

He stopped as if he had been shot, pointing with his left hand and clutching Limberham with his right.

Ahead of them, not more than fifty yards, had appeared a weird figure, fully six feet in height, black, gruesome, and spreading what appeared to be a pair of wings from its shoulders.

Then, with a cry that had little human in it, the figure turned and went bounding away.

"Stop!" shouted Townsend. "Man or fiend, I will know who you are!"

"Follow! Follow Spring-heeled Jack if you can!" came the mocking reply.

"Great Heaven!" Limberham gasped. "Is this a man we have to deal with?"

"We will see," Townsend said, drawing his pistol. "Ah! gone! By all that is wonderful—gone!"

"Over yonder wall, full ten feet high!" Limberham's voice cracked in his throat. "Did you not notice how silently and without effort the fiend rose? Townsend, what say you to this?"

"Ask me not now," the chief officer replied. "I am lost in amazement. But, be he man or fiend, yet will I stand face to face with Spring-heeled Jack!"

THE END.

You must not stop reading here. Buy the next number of the SPRING-HEELED JACK LIBRARY, now on sale at every newsagent's in the United Kingdom. It is entitled:

A MYSTERY OF MYSTERIES; or, Some Extraordinary Doings of Spring-Heeled Jack.

Now Ready.

Printed in Great Britain
by Amazon